MW00915943

DECEPTIVE
VICTORY

Also by J. E. Ribbey

The Last Patriots Series
American post-apocalyptic thrillers
Archangel
For You, My Dove
Rise of the Eagle
Operation Gray Owl

Young American Adventures
Middle grade historical fiction
The Innocent Rebel
Defiant Retreat
Under the Wing of the Storm
Deceptive Victory

Deceptive VICTORY

by J. E. RIBBEY

SORAYA JUBILEE PRESS
An imprint of The Jubilee Homestead LLC,
Stanchfield, Minnesota

Copyright © **2024 Joel and Esther Ribbey**

Visit the author's website at JERibbey.com

All rights reserved. No parts of this publication may be reproduced, stored in a retrieval system, or transmitted in any form or by any means, electronic, mechanical, photocopying, recording, or otherwise, without the prior written permission of the copyright owner.

Printed in the United States of America

LIBRARY OF CONGRESS CONTROL NUMBER: 2024913269

Print ISBN: 979-8-9899878-4-9
eBook ISBN: 979-8-9899878-5-6

Edited & cover design by Esther Ribbey

Cover image credit: Mary Hays at the Battle of Monmouth, original painting by Don Troiani, used with permission.

This is a work of fiction. Any similarity between the characters and situations within its pages and places or persons, living or dead, is unintentional and co-incidental.

To our own four young adventurers.

Chapter 1

April 28, 1778

Spring has returned, and I find the sun's rays warming me, body and soul. I feel as though I've aged a lifetime over the harsh winter; they are ever so costly. It isn't simply the cold, it's the bitter despair that settles over the camp as our brave soldiers are scarcely able to clothe themselves properly or find a meal to satisfy the gnawing in their stomachs. Congress says that French aid is on its way, but words do not feed a starving belly.

Still, as the weather warms, our spirits rise; the lack of warm clothing is forgotten, along with the cruelty of the fever, as folks turn their attention to a new season of planting, playing, and war. With the boys and the Bells back in camp, I've found myself rejoicing in the small things my soul longed for while they were away.

Adelaide and I have spent countless hours talking in hushed tones of all the goings on here and in Boston. She's sixteen now, and though she doesn't celebrate her birth, I wish I could have been there to let her know that I do. I truly hope I can, in turn, be the blessing that she is to me.

Benjamin seems to be of the same mind, and their relationship grows more dear by the day under Mrs. Bell's watchful eye. Adelaide puts on a brave face when he is called into the field, but I know she feels an awful ache that reaches deeper places than my own. We are neither of us foolish enough to believe that this war may not take more of our loved ones from us before it has had its fill.

Mrs. Bell has reopened her school for the camp children, and Adelaide and I are blessed to help whenever we can get away. I know it's a kindness to the families who are unable to read and write themselves. Even some of the soldiers find time to attend when they can. Having found her purpose has transformed her heart and Mrs. Bell seems right joyful to play her part.

Theo seems insistent on bringing his mate home every night, and I've had to place cotton in my ears on numerous occasions in order to sleep over the sound of their romantic chatter. He sleeps more during the day now, and he's lucky I allow him to, but as he seems smitten, there's little I can hold against him. Their nest is set in a hollow tree trunk only a stone's throw from our wagon. Once the young ones hatch, I'm sure I will be pestered to no end to feed them a constant *supply of rodents on account of Theo's lofty expectations. Abigail says she looks forward to the sure amusement of the matter.*

Even as I write, I can hear those two lovebirds hooting to one another over the soft dripping of a light spring rain. In the morning, we are sure to wake to a greener, brighter Valley Forge. Men will march on the green, birds will sing, and the sun will fill us all with new hope. There can't be a more wonderful season than spring.

Mercy Young, 15 years old.

Mercy smiled as she emerged from the wagon the following morning; she'd been right, the sun was shining, the grass was greener, and soldiers were already preparing for morning training on the green. She'd risen early, Theo had spent the majority of the night out hunting, and as such, she'd been able to sleep—a little. Stirring the coals in the fire ring, she was relieved to find a few still glowing. As quietly as she could, she reached for a couple pieces of dry kindling that were stacked under the wagon, kept safe from last night's rain.

"Morning, Mercy," 11-year-old David groaned from his hammock, hanging just over the pile.

"Morning, Dave."

"Are you fixin' some breakfast? I'm hungrier than a bear."

"We don't have much . . . I could make firecakes and some salted pork."

"A starving man is happy to have anything," Abe sighed from his hammock. At thirteen, starving was his normal condition.

"Then we all ought to be thankful," David replied.

"Indeed," Abigail said, emerging from the wagon.

"Morning, Mama," Mercy said.

"Good morning, my blessings," Abigail replied. "Give me a minute, Mercy, and I'll help you get things prepared."

"I'll find you some more firewood," Abe volunteered, climbing out of bed.

"Thank you," Mercy replied.

In moments, the dried kindling began to smoke from the heat of the coals, and after a few sharp puffs from David, it burst into flames.

"You're getting pretty good at that," Mercy said.

David nodded. "I'll go fetch some water from the river."

"Thank you," Mercy called after him. "Don't come back with any frogs this time!"

The last time he'd gone to fetch the water, he'd captured a small frog slowed by the morning chill, and with no other place to put it, and the pail being heavy as it was, he'd simply plopped it in the water and forgot about it. Poor thing would have ended up in the kettle if Abe hadn't spotted it. Abigail had made poor

David wash the water pail four times before she was satisfied the water wasn't tainted. It was good to have them back.

In a half hour, the four of them sat around a crackling fire eating a bland breakfast with gratefulness.

"I heard that dreadful, crafty General Howe has resigned and sailed back to England," Abigail said. "Capt. Davis said it was on account he'd failed to whip us before the French joined the war. There's a new general in charge of the redcoats now, a man named General Henry Clinton. He's a veteran of many a war."

"Won't matter," Abe said with a shrug. "It's two countries against one; we're surely going to beat them now, and I'll have missed my chance."

"Let it be, Lord Jesus," Abigail prayed out loud.

"Haven't you seen enough war, Abe?" Mercy asked.

"Seein' it and fightin' it are two different things," Abe countered. "A man's got to find out if he's got the salt to stand in the face of the enemy, or the question will haunt him all the days of his life."

"Who filled your head with that nonsense?" Abigail demanded.

"Why Mr. Hadley, of course. He says every man's got the question burnin' deep down, and it needs answerin'."

"Mercy, remind me the next time we see that man that I am cross with him," Abigail said.

"Yes, ma'am," Mercy replied, fighting to hide a smirk.

"And what about you, David, are you chomping at the bit to get yourself blown to pieces too?" Abigail asked.

David looked up from his plate, glancing over at Abraham and then back to Abigail. "Well . . . I am a man, Mama," he said, swallowing hard. "Though I don't fancy myself getting blown up."

"You don't, do you?" Abigail chuffed. "Well, let's hope the enemy asks your permission first!"

Again, David swallowed hard. "Perhaps I'm not as itchin' as Abe."

"Let's pray we don't need to find out," Abigail said, relaxing a bit. "I wish those Frenchmen would get a move on."

"Have you heard anything about when Henry and Ben might be coming back?" Mercy asked.

"They're off foraging again, so it's unlikely they've gone far. Between the redcoats and the Continentals, it's a miracle folks around here have enough to live on themselves," Abigail mused.

"The waters of the Schuylkill have cleared up since the snow melt; perhaps we could try some fishing this afternoon once our work and school are finished," Abe offered.

"It would be nice to have fresh food for a change," Abigail agreed. "But stay close to camp, and no capturing British soldiers this time."

"Mama, that happened one time. . . . We wouldn't do something that foolish twice," Mercy balked.

"No, I suppose not," Abigail said, getting up and collecting everyone's dishes. "This time you'll come home with a wildcat you aim to tame."

Mercy caught an excited gleam in David's eye but held up her hand to stop his rebuttal. Collecting the rest of the dishes, she followed Abigail to the stream. The water still held the winter's chill, and her fingers went numb as she scrubbed the frypan.

"You're a good mama," Mercy said, as they scrubbed. "I thank the Lord every day that you and Papa Henry were good enough to take us in."

"I scarcely remember a time before you were in my life," Abigail replied. "It's as though you've always been a part of me. As a little girl I only ever had one dream . . . being a mother. I thought the Lord had taken it from me, but he'd just had another way. If Henry and I had children of our own, we may not have had room for you, and that is a thought that breaks my heart. I understand now, he was saving a place for you."

Mercy looked up through grateful tears, and Abigail placed a gentle kiss on her head.

"You, Mercy Young, are my feisty, scrappy, hardworking daughter, and I am proud to call you such."

Setting down her dishes, Mercy folded into Abigail. She was no longer the soft round woman they'd met in Cambridge. The war had transformed her figure into a lean, hard, strong frame, but even so, in Abigail's arms was Mercy's favorite place to be.

Chapter 2

Water swirled lazily by as the Youngs and their friends, the Bells, soaked in the afternoon rays by the river's edge. Abe took on the role of preparing the girls' canes for fishing. A few plump spring worms had been plucked from their homes under a rotted log to serve as bait.

Mercy chose to forgo a cork, and instead used split shot to keep her line on the bottom. Everywhere they'd traveled with the army had provided new rivers, ponds, and harbors to fish. Each was its own unique challenge, and they'd learned a lot through trial and error, and the sage advice of soldier passersby who'd had some experience in those types of waters.

There was always a mystery and anticipation about fishing. You never knew what kinds of scaly creatures lurked under the water's surface. Some were shiny and some dull, some had pretty colors, spots, or stripes, and some were simply silver, some had whiskers, or both eyes on one side of their head, some were small, while others would break the line or nearly drag a person in!

"Why aren't you using a cane, Abe?" Nathaniel Bell, Adelaide's twelve-year-old brother, asked.

"I'm using a spool like this, with some heavier shot, so I can toss my line further out into the deeper water," Abe replied.

"Why?" Nathaniel asked again.

"Because, if we only fish as far as our canes can reach, we'll never know what kinds of fish live out there in the deeper water. Who knows, there could be monsters."

"I wanna catch a monster," David piped up.

"I said there *could* be monsters . . . I'll have to catch one to know for sure."

The six of them set up along the shore; Mercy and Adelaide fished beside one another in a small eddy laying back restfully against the bank with their canes propped up by forked sticks. David and Nathaniel, always competitive, hardly left their worms in the water for more than a few moments before determining the spot baren of fish and racing off to try another. Mable and Abe sat on opposite ends of a large log waiting patiently for something to bite.

They'd only been fishing a short while when Mercy noticed a familiar shadow circling above her. Sure enough, Theo had spotted them with their canes from his nesting tree and had come to pillage. He landed gracefully beside her and hopped withing arms reach so she could stroke his tufted head.

"Are you a papa yet?" Mercy asked, indulging him.

"He must be," Adelaide said. "His family is eating more than we are. I gave him a whole nest of mice I found in a crate of bandages we overlooked somehow."

"I got one!" yelled David, holding up his line with a small silvery fish hanging from it.

"That's a tiny one . . . it should only count as half," hollered Nathaniel.

"A fish is a fish!" shouted David. "That's one to nothing!"

"Bring it over here," hollered Abe.

"Why? It's too tiny to keep."

"Theo likes the small ones," Mercy said.

"He can have the next one," Abe said. "I want to use it as bait."

David brought the little fish over and handed it to Abe. "How are you gonna hook it on?"

"Poor thing," Mable said.

"What's the difference if I use it for bait or Theo eats it? It's dead either way."

"I don't know, feeding Theo at least gives it a purpose," Mable replied.

"It's *going* to have a purpose," Abe said, hooking the small fish just in front of its tail. "I'm going to catch an even bigger fish with it." He tossed his line back into the river where the little fish disappeared beneath the ripples.

Theo ruffled his feathers in frustration.

"It's okay, we'll catch you another one," Mercy reassured him confidently.

The afternoon proved productive for Theo, but little else. Each of them caught several small silvery fish but nothing worth bringing home to camp, everyone except Abe, who continued to wait. The sun was beginning to dip and Mercy knew they needed to start back to the wagon to prepare for another lean meal when Abe's line began to move.

His twine shifted where it met the water so subtly it was hardly noticeable, but little by little it began to creep its way upstream against the current.

Abe stood from the log as his fingers tested the line. "It doesn't feel right, there's no sharp strike, just a steady heavy pull. . . ."

"Aren't you gonna set the hook?" Mercy asked.

Abe nodded, slowly winding the last bit of slack line around his dowel. When the line was taut, he gave it a swift jerk.

"AWE!" Abe said, kicking the sand. "I think it's caught on something." He jerked it this way and that, attempting to free it, and then, all of a sudden, it pulled back! "Mercy . . ." his voice quivered.

The creature pulled again, and Abe's eyes grew wide. Then it made a run upstream, only it wasn't a fast run, more like . . . a powerful crawl. Abe was drug to the water's edge before he loosened his grip and let the line spool slowly from the dowel. He tracked the creature, following it along the bank. The rest of them brought in their lines and took off after him.

"It's got to be a whale or something," David said, as they caught up with Abe.

"It feels like there's a horse on the other end," Abe grunted.

After about forty yards, the creature stopped. Abe pulled on the line, and the creature pulled back. Abe pulled harder, winding a little bit of line at a time around his dowel. The creature on the other end tugged defiantly, but Abe was beginning to gain the upper hand. Inches at a time, he added new twine to the dowel, the creature feeling more like dead weight than a fish.

Eerily, a large dark figure appeared in the water only a dozen feet from shore. A few more feet and a hideous beaked head emerged from the water, hissing and snapping at the air.

"What on earth is that?!" Adelaide exclaimed.

"I didn't know you meant a real monster!" Mable said, ducking behind Adelaide.

"I—I think it's a turtle," Abe said, hauling the thrashing creature to shore.

It was dark and muddy, with large, thick, powerful legs equipped with long sharp claws. Its tail was long and bumpy like its neck. Its head had two beady eyes, and a large sharply beaked mouth that hissed and snapped with fury. And what's worse, it smelled terrible, like a rotting corpse.

"If it is, that's the ugliest turtle I've ever seen," Mercy said.

"I think I'm going to be sick," Mable groaned.

"Do you think we can eat it?" Abe asked.

"I don't think I could," Adelaide answered, holding her stomach at the thought.

Abe frowned. "Well, I guess I'll try and get my hook back and let it go. Abigail will never believe this story."

Abe took a step towards the creature, whose head shot out like a snake and took a snap at him. "Good Lord!" Abe exclaimed, jumping back.

"Maybe you can try getting round behind it," David offered.

Abe moved around behind the critter and again took a step towards it. This time the turtle extended its neck the length of its entire shell and took a snap at him again, before pivoting its body around to face him.

Abe looked over at Mercy placing his hand on his chest, perplexed.

"Maybe try getting it to bite something, then, while it's busy chewing on that, you can get your hook back," Mercy suggested.

Abe fetched a cane, extending the thicker end towards his quarry. When the hilt was within striking distance, the creature lunged and snapped down hard, cutting the cane clean off.

Everyone gasped.

Abe stared at the cane in shock; it'd been thicker than his thumb. Sliding his knife from his pocket, he flicked out his blade and cut his line without giving it another thought. The creature drug itself back to the water's edge and slipped in, leaving a considerable wake behind it.

"I don't think I want to catch any monsters," David said, as they watched it go.

Back at the wagon everyone took turns telling the details of the adventure to Abigail and Mrs. Bell from their perspective. By the time they were done, Abigail had added one more creature to her list of detestables and praised Abe for having the good sense to give up his hook rather than his hand.

As Mercy lay writing it all out by candlelight, she found she rather admired the hideous beast. It was powerful, well-armed, and armored; it had to be the king of its dark domain. It had no need to be fast, it could clearly defend itself, it was never away from home, and if it wanted something, it could probably just take it. Though it did add a bit of anxiety to any future swims.

Chapter 3

By early May, the weather had warmed significantly, and the medical staff gained the upper hand over the fever. The camp was filled with the sounds of training from sunup to sundown, while Henry and her older brother, Benjamin's, light rifleman unit was constantly deployed to keep an eye on General Clinton and the redcoats in Philadelphia.

Washington seemed content to watch and wait, keeping the redcoat foraging parties in check rather than confronting the whole of the British army directly, at least not before French supplies and reinforcements arrived.

Congress promised financial aid was on the way, and the army would at last be paid after a year without wages. This news, along with the notion that, with French support the war would soon be over, bolstered the Continental ranks with young new soldiers not wanting to miss their chance at participating in this glorious fight. A notion Mercy knew would fade to nothing during their first skirmish.

Abigail hoped the king would simply recognize that the contest no longer leaned in his favor and quit, but Henry said the French only evened the playing field at best. The redcoats had even more to gain now. If they won, they would prove their global dominance yet again. They also had more to lose; a loss to the rebellion in the colonies could lead to rebellion all across the empire. The fighting from here on was sure to be careful and calculated.

Everyone waited. With each passing day the tension grew as spies on either side delivered intelligence to clever generals and strategists. Two armies, circling one another like tomcats, searching for weakness and opportunity, a chance to score a blow to their opponent's soft underbelly. The life and death of a nation hanging in the balance.

There was little time left before the promised French reinforcements arrived, the redcoats needed to strike soon. Washington's army, on the other hand, needed only to survive. The move was General Clinton's to make.

"I wish I knew when Ben would be returning," Adelaide said, as she, Mercy, and Abigail sat sipping tea during their noon break.

"I suspect it'll be today," Abigail said. "They only brought three days rations with them this time."

"That's clever," Adelaide said.

"There's more than one way to get information." Abigail smiled.

"You could be a spy," Mercy laughed.

"And give up all this?" Abigail said, gesturing to the medical tent. "Besides, I've heard Washington has a whole network of spies passing him information from New York and Philadelphia. Good folks, risking their lives. The redcoats hang spies."

"I think it would be exciting to be a spy," Mercy said. "I love hearing things I know I'm not supposed to."

"Mercy!" Abigail gasped. "That's the kind of talk that could land you in real danger. It's best to keep to yourself and your work, there's no need to be inviting that kind of trouble."

"I'm only getting your dander up, Mama," Mercy smiled. "I was just teasing—mostly."

"Lord, have mercy," Abigail said, placing her hand on her heart. "It's no wonder my hair is turning gray. . . ."

Abigail's suspicion proved correct when Henry and Benjamin rode into camp later that afternoon, and Capt. Davis graciously gave the girls the rest of the afternoon off to spend with their loved ones. In order to share Benjamin with Adelaide, Abigail cleverly invited the Bells for supper that evening.

"It's true," Henry said as they ate. "The redcoats in Philadelphia are disguising their intentions well. The city is not easily defended, they must know that staying there with the French on their way would spell destruction."

"You're saying they must give up the city or risk losing the war?" Abigail asked.

"That's my assessment." Henry nodded.

"Where would they go?" Abe asked.

"Back to New York, I suspect. It's much simpler to supply and defend."

"It would be nice to see the redcoats retreating for a change," Mercy said.

"Aye," Henry agreed.

"When will the French get here?" David asked.

"Not for another month, I'm told," Henry replied. "And that's only if the British don't engage them at sea."

"Fighting season will be half over by then," Ben said.

"We'll have to hold out."

The fire's light danced majestically off the wagon and the host of resolute faces surrounding its flames. Mercy caught Mrs. Bell smiling to herself as she watched Ben and Adelaide, and when Mercy followed her gaze, she understood why. The night had grown long, and in the comfort of having him home, Adelaide's exhausted heart had finally found rest. Her head rested gently on his shoulder; her eyes closed in contented sleep.

Adelaide felt no need to know the ins and outs of the war, only that her love was safe and sound, and that she was safe with him. The exhaustion she felt was that of love parted, and the rest it required was here now. She'd absorb all she could, and then, when the orders came, let him go again. Even Mrs. Bell could see the mercy in letting her be.

Mercy smiled too. It gave her hope, hope that life would continue beyond the war, and love would continue to blossom and grow. Broken people, people who'd seen and done difficult things, would find each other and together, by God's grace, they'd heal, start over, and make something new. A new world.

Benjamin and Henry had only been home for four days when they were ordered to march out on May 18th with the Marquis de Lafayette and a twenty-one-hundred-man battalion whose aim was to set up overlooking Philadelphia to harass a British exodus from the city.

Abigail clung to Henry for as long as she could, and Adelaide refused to leave Benjamin's side. This wasn't a foraging parting or a scouting mission; this was the first march of the spring campaign. As much as Mercy enjoyed the romance of Ben and Adelaide's relationship, she didn't envy them. The heartache and worry were more than she wanted to bear at this time in her life.

There were plenty of boys in camp, but she'd made sure they understood they'd survive longer if they *didn't* show an interest in her.

Mercy said her goodbyes, said her prayers, and went back to work. Her patients kept her mind off the "what ifs" and allowed her to carry out each day without the constant agony of fretting about her loved ones. It wasn't that she didn't worry—she did, but she'd realized the worry couldn't change anything. They were in the Lord's hands.

"They're off to war again," Capt. Davis said as the drummers' cadence marched the battalion out of camp.

"The fighting had to start some time," Mercy replied.

"Washington has ordered that every commander act with prudence. Victory is finally within reach; the king won't be able to hold out for long against our army and the French. He's demanded that all caution be taken so providence is not squandered by carelessness. I'm sure Lafayette will carry out this order to the letter, your family is in good hands."

"I didn't think you liked the 'French Peacock.'" Mercy said.

Capt. Davis cleared his throat uncomfortably. "It—it turns out my misgivings were simply a matter of cultural differences."

"Huh, looked like jealousy to me."

Capt. Davis's cheeks flushed. "Jealous?! Of him? Ha! It wouldn't even be a fair contest. . . . Why, if it wasn't for his rank, which was simply given to ingratiate the French, with whom he is very well connected, I would be his superior. No, I'm afraid I rather look upon him as a sibling—yes, I see him as I would a younger brother."

"Ah, is that right. And the fact he has nearly every girl in camp fawning after him had nothing to do with it?"

"Every girl?" Capt. Davis asked, lifting an eyebrow.

"I said nearly," Mercy corrected.

"It doesn't bother me in the slightest," Capt. Davis continued. "Who in their right mind would want to venture into the murky waters of a courtship at a time like this?"

"That makes two of us," Mercy said.

"There! You, see? I was never jealous of General Lafayette."

Mercy studied her grinning opponent for a moment, before shaking her head in defeat. "Consider my accusation withdrawn," Mercy said, extending her hand.

"Done," Capt. Davis said, taking her hand and shaking it. "No offense taken," he said, puffing out his chest. "I hear young ladies are prone to having wild imaginations about these sorts of things."

Mercy rolled her eyes. "I'm going to get back to my patients."

Capt. Davis gave her a courteous bow.

Mercy stifled a snort as she walked away. Who was acting like a peacock now?

Chapter 4

May 20, 1778

Tonight I write with a grateful heart; Ben and Papa were just this morning set upon by an overwhelming British force nearly triple their number. The redcoats had coyly encircled their position on Barren Hill during the night, where General Lafayette was keeping an eye on Philadelphia. At daybreak they attacked the hill, thinking they had the Americans dead to rights, but General Lafayette knew of another way off the hill, through some low ground hidden by the ridge, and they were able to escape.

A rider said they were in a hopeless situation, but providence showed them the way. While the outcome is worth rejoicing, the attack itself proves our enemy is not yet ready to board their ships and go home. Three men gave their lives as part of the rear guard, and a party of Oneida Indians ambushed the redcoats who gave pursuit, providing the army time to retreat. They are the real heroes.

Lafayette's army will be returning to camp to come up with a new plan much sooner than we had expected; news we are all excited to hear. It'll only be for a little while, and then they'll be gone again, but so long as they always come back, I've learned to be content.

Capt. Davis informed us that Washington wants the entire camp ready to move at all times. When the redcoats leave Philadelphia, he intends to engage them on the road. All our supplies have been packed in crates so they can be loaded in a hurry. It is tedious at times trying to search for things, and I've grown quite flustered on a number of occasions these past few days when I can't find what I'm looking for. The generals have no idea what it takes to render proper aid, nor do they bear the inconveniences they've pressed upon us.

I'd like nothing more than to barge into Washington's tent and box up all of his things, but Abigail says that is a bitter notion, and I ought to be more understanding. I feel something of the kind would make the generals more understanding, but apparently that is not a fifteen-year-old girl's place. I'd probably be court martialed and hung, which would be a tragedy because Theo and his family would probably starve to death. In light of that, I should probably take Abigail's advice and refrain.

I hope Lafayette arrives tomorrow; the camp is always lively when brothers-in-arms come back together. There is a meekness in learning to celebrate the little things; it seems to make life purer in some way.

We are all in this struggle together, we mourn together, and we rejoice together; and this escape is something to celebrate.

May God keep all my family, until we can be together again.

Mercy Young, 15 years old.

By midafternoon the following day, Lafayette marched his men back into Valley Forge, little the worse for wear. Henry, Benjamin, and the rest of their unit were released to their families and friends, and the camp was soon filled with exciting tales of Lafayette's daring escape.

"We'd never have dared to hope we'd have you back so soon," Abigail beamed, clinging to Henry's arm. "Seems they sent you on a fool's errand."

"Not a fool's errand," Henry replied. "The trip was rather enlightening. General Clinton is clearly a shrewd leader, with good intelligence. He'd have had us all if the general hadn't guided us so tactfully off that hill. General Washington will have to be equally calculating if we are to make full use of our advantage."

"What's the Frenchman like?" David asked.

"He took great care with us, not willing to part with a single one if he could help it. He is wise for his youth, and though I could sense the hunger for battle in him, he had the prudence to see that retreat would deal the greater blow. We are fortunate to have him."

"I think he sounds funny," David said.

"He does take a little getting used to," Henry said, ruffling David's hair.

"Well, the army got to stretch its legs at any rate," Abigail added.

"Aye," Henry agreed. "It was good practice, and the army proved its composure under difficult circumstances. The longer the war goes on, the better we become. General Clinton has a far more difficult task than his predecessor."

"Aren't you going to tell them?" Benjamin prompted Henry with a grin.

"Tell us what?" Abe asked.

Henry stopped, straightening his coat. "I've ... been promoted to sergeant."

"Congratulations!" Mercy said, giving him a hug. "You deserve it."

"Benjamin has been placed under my command, with a dozen other riflemen."

"You're a fine leader," Abigail said, giving him a peck on the cheek. "They're lucky to have you."

"You don't sound like a sergeant," David said. "They all shout orders like they've got gravel stuck in their throats."

"I guess I'll have to work on that," Henry smiled. "Now go get some kindling for this fire at the double!" he barked.

"Yes, sir!" David saluted, racing off to find some sticks.

"Not bad," Benjamin said. "A bit soft though."

"It was my first time," Henry replied, clearing his throat.

"Alright," Abigail said, hooking their arms. "Let's get you two famished soldiers something to eat."

The camp atmosphere filled with the sounds of hopeful conversations, and the sweet smell of pipe smoke. When they'd finished supper, Henry produced a deck of cards he'd picked up on their travels and set about teaching everyone a game called Whist he and Benjamin had learned from their comrades to pass the time.

The game required two teams to play, and after some convincing that there would be no gambling, Adelaide was allowed to team up with Benjamin, while Mercy joined Henry. The cards were dealt, and the family gathered round. Mercy had no idea a game could come with so much pressure, there were so many unknowns, so many possibilities, and she had no idea what cards Henry possessed.

After losing the first trick, it only got worse. Henry reassured her they were alright, but she felt like she'd let him down. Benjamin played a card, and she searched her hand for a better one. Nervously placing a queen, her heart sank as Adelaide placed a king. Henry looked up at her reassuringly and winked, then he placed an ace, winning the trick.

Mercy breathed a sigh of relief; it was one trick to one. Everyone watched with bated breath as each team traded tricks round after round. It was five tricks each when Adelaide played a nine. Henry was unable to match the suit and played an off-suit two instead. Benjamin grinned as he threw down an ace. It was Mercy's turn. She only had a couple cards in her hand, but one of them was a trump card. Ignoring Ben, she placed the trump card with feigned indifference.

"Argh," Ben grumbled as Mercy swept the trick in front of her.

"Last trick," Henry said.

Mercy placed her last card, a ten, and Benjamin beat it with a jack. Her heart drummed in her chest as Henry scratched his chin for a moment.

"Oh, for crying out loud," Ben complained. "You've only got one card left, just play it!"

"As you wish," Henry said, laying down a trump card.

Mercy gasped.

Adelaide frowned, laying down a queen.

"We won!" Henry smiled.

"Rats!" Ben said. "You got lucky, but that was only the first round."

"There's another round?!" Mercy cried. "I don't know if my heart can take it."

"Nor mine," Abigail said.

The boys watched in awe as Henry shuffled the cards several times, it seemed like magic. He promised to help them practice when they were done with their game.

It took three more rounds of Whist before the game was through. In the end, Benjamin and Adelaide were able to secure victory. There were many laughs at the near continual parrying banter between Henry and Ben, and by the end of the game Mercy was able to relax and enjoy the blessing of it. Abigail on the other hand, refused to play the next game on account the whole process left her stomach in knots.

By the time they went to sleep that night, the boys were shuffling cards, Mercy had won a game on Abe's team, and everyone felt full. They were safe, together, and free; Mercy couldn't think of anything she needed beyond that.

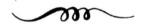

In the morning Henry and Ben went to drill on the green, Mercy, Adelaide, and Abigail went to work at the medical tent, and the younger children attended school with Mrs. Bell. That was normal life now, a good day, if the redcoats didn't spoil it, and it was plenty to be thankful for.

As she tended to a patient, she heard Capt. Davis conversing just outside the back flap of the tent. Her conscience told her to ignore it and keep working, that it wasn't her place to eavesdrop, and reminded her of the last time he'd caught her listening above her station, but . . .

Finishing with her patient, she *accidently* dropped her ladle and watched it bounce predictably towards the flap. Innocently she stepped closer to retrieve it.

"I've got nothing for you, all the demanding in the world isn't going to change that," Capt. Davis said in a pleading tone.

He sounded distressed.

"You should know that impeding an officer in his work is a punishable offense." He continued. "The rules of the army apply to everyone in the camp."

Someone was really getting under his skin.

"If you'd just permit me, I'd go inside and fetch her!"

Fetch her? Mercy leaned in to hear more.

"Listen, you blasted bird! I'm telling you, she's just inside!"

Mercy gasped, sweeping aside the flap to see a very frazzled Capt. Davis shaking his fist at Theo, who looked up from near her feet.

"At last," he sighed. "I was about to fetch a musket," he said, glaring at Theo.

"Are you okay, Theo?" Mercy cooed, squatting down beside him. "Don't listen to a word he says, he'd never harm a feather on your head."

"Is *he* okay?!" Capt. Davis balked. "I've been held hostage by this bandit for the better part of a quarter hour!"

"I'll bet you're just hungry, aren't you?" Mercy continued. "Parenting is hard work, isn't it?"

"*Please*," Capt. Davis scoffed. "There is nothing difficult in that pathetic creature's life."

Mercy lifted the lid on a nearby crock revealing a mouse she'd caught earlier in the day. Carefully, she tipped it out at Theo's feet, where he pounced on it the moment it leapt from the container. He looked up at Mercy as if to say thank you, and then flapped his wings and flew back towards his nest.

"How can you expect him to like you if you treat him like that?" Mercy asked.

"I have no need of a bird's affections, just his respect," Capt. Davis countered.

"Affection or respect; I think the only way you're getting on his good side is through his stomach," Mercy said, standing back up.

"That bird is a tyrant, and you've made him so."

Mercy looked at the ground.

"Though, he is a charming little tyrant *most* of the time."

Mercy lifted her head, and Capt. Davis gave her a soft smile. "Come on, let's get on with our duties."

Following him back inside, Mercy smiled to herself; Capt. Davis was developing a soft spot for Theo. She wasn't sure why it mattered to her, only that it did, and it made her glad to know that they were getting along. She couldn't wait to share the silly story with Adelaide when she brought her soiled rags out to the cauldron. Thanks to Theo, she'd have something to write about today.

Chapter 5

Mercy awoke from a rare night's rest on June 6th after a week of almost constant hooting. Theo's offspring had outgrown the nest and, following a week of amusing flying practice, had finally flown off to establish territories of their own. To say the racket had nearly driven them all mad was hardly an overstatement. Even the ever-merciful Abigail had sworn she'd learn to shoot a musket if it didn't stop soon. Even Theo seemed relieved by their departure and hardly cracked an eye as she climbed down from the buckboard.

The sun was just beginning to rise, a warm southern breeze whispered of a hot day ahead. Holding her hand over the fire ring, she found the coals had all died out during the night. Collecting kindling from under the wagon, she used a bit of cotton and a few twigs and placed them in the center of the ring.

Then she took the kindling hatchet from the side of the wagon and a flint and struck the flint over the cotton. A shower of sparks flew from the rock, landing amongst the cotton fibers causing it to smolder. Blowing on it softly, it burst into flames, consuming the cotton and igniting the twigs.

She added several smaller pieces of kindling to the small flame and waited a moment for them to catch before adding more. If she added them too quickly, she'd put it out; she'd had that misfortune before. Slowly the fire grew until she was able to add two split pieces of firewood. Once she was sure it wouldn't go out, she picked up the water pail and headed for the river.

On her way she passed several soldiers emerging from their cabins preparing to start the day. They nodded to her politely, and she returned the gesture with a sort of moving curtsy. Many of them, she assumed, had been under her care at one time or another, though there were far too many of them now for her to remember any but the most horrifying or interesting cases.

As she dipped the pail into the river, she studied her reflection in the water. Her childlikeness was gone, her once rounded cheeks replaced by a sharp jawline; she really did look like her mother. They hadn't had the money before she died to have her portrait painted like some of the wealthy folks, but now, she knew she'd always find her in her own reflection.

"I love you, Mama," Mercy said. "Tell Papa, if you can, that we're doing fine, and that we miss him always."

She lifted the pail from the water and started back to camp to wake the boys. When she arrived, she was relieved to find Benjamin already up and dressing for drill. She set down the pail and picked up a semi-pointed bit of kindling.

"Rise and shine boys," she said cheerfully, giving each of their hammocks a gentle shake.

David groaned and rolled over, while Abe still slept like the dead.

"Boys!" she said, shaking their hammocks again.

"What?!" snarled David.

"Go away!" groaned Abe.

Mercy looked at Benjamin and held up the stick. He looked back mournfully but nodded all the same.

Mercy took aim at the bulge in the canvas made by Abe's buttocks and lunged forward like a fencer in a duel.

"OUCH!" Abe cried, sitting bolt upright and drilling his head into the bottom of the wagon so hard he fell clean out of his hammock.

Mercy gasped, cupping her hands over her mouth.

"Darn it, Mercy!" Abe shouted, rubbing his head. "What'd you do that for?!"

She watched as a large goose egg began to rise on his forehead.

"Sorry Abe, I guess you should'a got up the first time I told you," Mercy winced.

"I'm up!" David said, sitting up and hopping out of his hammock. "No need to poke me."

"Good," Mercy replied. "Abigail put me in charge, and we're already burning daylight. You boys get after your chores while I fix up some breakfast."

"Can't even let us get a little sleep while Abigail and Henry are away. . . ." Abe muttered. "We're not slaves you know!"

Henry had elected to take Abigail on his run to the tavern to give her a break from the owls, and probably keep her from doing something rash. They'd set out the day before and expected to be gone about a week. Abigail had nearly called the whole thing off with worry, imagining all the possible ways the children would find to endanger themselves while they were away, but Henry had insisted that they'd learned many a valuable lesson over the years, and as such were surely more cautious than most children their age.

It was with great reluctance that Abigail had climbed into the wagon, but her fatigue on account of the owls had dulled her resistance. Even as the wagon pulled away, Mercy could still hear Henry reassuring her the children would be okay.

And they would be. Mercy had everything well in hand. There wasn't a situation that could arise that she couldn't handle after all they'd been through. Besides, if the boys got out of hand, Mrs. Bell offered to let them stay with her. A fate she wouldn't wish on anyone.

Mercy collected the frypan and set to work making some firecakes; they'd have fish later if the boys could manage some success that afternoon. Firecakes were no culinary treat, just flower and salt, hardly enough to take the edge off. Hopefully Abigail and Henry would bring back some other ingredients, butter and potatoes, perhaps an onion or garlic, or even a cabbage.

Her stomach gnawed on itself thinking of all the delicious combinations they'd be able to create with just a few more ingredients. A little seasoning could turn a mundane meal into a pleasurable experience, and Abigail always said that God gave them the ability to taste so that they could enjoy the pleasure of his provision.

Mercy placed the first two firecakes in Ben's knapsack and tied it closed.

"Thank you, Mercy. I best be off," he said, giving her a hug. "Don't be too hard on them."

"I won't. You take care of yourself."

Ben nodded and trotted off to meet with his company for roll call. Their papa would be proud if he could see him now. The boy who'd left Lexington now shaved with a razor, though his face had suffered considerable damage the first time Henry had taught him, and he wore a fine military uniform. His hair was pulled back and held in place by a black bow beneath a black military hat. He looked as soldierly as any of them as he disappeared over the hill, rifle in hand.

David returned with an armload of kindling and added it to the pile under the wagon. "Can we eat now? My stomach's so hungry I feel I'm going to be sick."

"Go collect Abe from his splitting and get washed up. I'll have the firecakes ready by then."

When the boys returned, Abe said grace, and they ate their meager breakfast with gratefulness. The swelling on Abe's head had gone down some, but it had turned purple and looked mighty tender as it pulsed each time he chewed his food.

"I've got to be off to the medical tent soon, you boys make your way over to the Bells and conduct your schoolin'," Mercy said.

"Mercy, we've been doing that every day without anyone saying a word, what makes you think you need to tell us today?" David complained.

"Yeah, just because Abigail put you in charge doesn't make you our mama," Abe added.

"Just see to it you're there," Mercy said. "Mrs. Bell—"

"We'll be there," Abe said, rolling his eyes.

"I'm just trying to do a good job," Mercy muttered, taking their plates.

"And so are we," Abe said.

"I know," Mercy said. "I'm sorry. I'll see you boys this afternoon when I finish with my patients, maybe we can go on an adventure."

"Can we bring the Bells?" David asked.

"Of course," Mercy replied.

After cleaning up breakfast, Mercy walked over to the medical tent. Adelaide met her on the way and instantly Mercy felt the weight of her morning melting away.

"Where are you coming from?" Mercy asked.

Adelaide blushed. "I got up early so I could meet Ben and walk with him to the green."

"Ahhh," Mercy smiled.

"He's so handsome in his uniform," Adelaide smiled.

"He is that," Mercy agreed.

"He's grander than Lafayette to my eyes," Adelaide said.

Mercy shook her head. "You're smitten. And you'd better not tell him that or he'll be strutting round here like a barnyard rooster. Abigail says that a pretty girl gives a boy a strange kind of confidence, he's likely to try any fool thing."

"I'd like to see that," Adelaide grinned.

"Adelaide!" Mercy gasped. "Come on, let's get you to work before you're completely undone."

Mercy shook her head to herself while she worked. What had gotten into her friend? The Adelaide she'd met would have been red as a tomato just to think those things let alone say them! If she ever got the notion to feel romantically inclined, she'd make sure never to depart from her right mind during the process.

"Something the matter, Mercy?" Capt. Davis asked.

"Uh, no, sir," Mercy replied sheepishly.

"You were shaking your head."

"Just thinking to myself. I've got a lot on my mind with Henry and Abigail gone for the week."

"Ahh, that is a lot of responsibility, especially with two younger brothers. I'm sure you are more than capable of handling things until they return. You're probably one of the most capable young ladies I've had the pleasure of meeting."

Mercy's face flushed. "You're very capable too, sir."

"Uh, thank you," Capt. Davis replied awkwardly. "I'd better get back to my duty."

As he walked away, Mercy ran her palm down her face. *You're very capable too?! What is wrong with you, Mercy? He pays you a compliment about being competent and you respond like a daft idiot. All you had to say was thank you.*

Mercy shook it from her mind, she could work it out in her diary later. She didn't know what'd come over her; chalking it up to a stressful morning without coffee, she continued on with her patients.

When they'd finished making their rounds, Mercy and Adelaide walked nonchalantly back towards the wagons, stopping for a bit to watch the soldiers marching on the green. Mercy smiled as she watched her friend search the faces of the soldiers, looking for Ben. When they'd concluded his unit was not amongst those practicing, they continued on their way.

Nearing their wagon, Mercy thought she smelled the familiar smell of Henry's pipe smoke, but that couldn't be, they weren't going to be back for at least six more days. By the time they reached the wagon, she was sure she smelled it, but there was no one in sight. She looked at Adelaide.

"I smell it too," Adelaide whispered.

Carefully, Mercy climbed up onto the buckboard and threw open the canvas flap just as David was about to take a puff. David gasped, inhaling deeply. Mercy watched as he turned red, and then green, before erupting into a coughing fit. Beside him sat Nathaniel Bell, looking as though he'd been caught with his hand in the cookie jar. Abraham was nowhere to been seen.

Adelaide jumped up into the buckboard beside her as Mercy stood frozen in shock.

"Nathaniel Bell!" Adelaide exclaimed.

"I'm dying, Mercy," David wheezed as tears began rolling down his cheeks. "I can't breathe—I can't breathe."

Mercy clambered in beside him. "Slow down, just slow down. Small breaths, Dave."

David gasped in her arms, beginning to turn purple. Mercy rubbed his back trying to calm him.

"It burns!" he coughed.

Little by little his panicked breaths grew deeper and longer until it appeared he was through the worst of it.

"I-I thought I was going to die," he said in a raspy voice.

"What were you thinking David?!" Mercy asked.

Dave looked at his feet. "We found Henry's spare pipe and a bit of tobacco. It always smells so nice when he smokes it. . . . We—we just wanted to try it."

"Do you see any other boys your age smoking pipes?!" Mercy asked.

David shook his head.

"And as for you!" Adelaide said, grabbing Nathaniel by the ear and twisting it. "You're the older one! You should've advised against this."

"It was his idea," David moaned.

Adelaide wrenched Nathaniel's ear so hard, Mercy half expected it to come off. Nathaniel let out a shrill howl and glared at David for his betrayal.

"We're going straight to Mama, and you'd better start beggin' the Lord's mercy!" Adelaide said, dragging him from the wagon by the ear.

Mercy could hear him yelping all the way to the Bell's wagon.

"I'm real sorry, Mercy. I shouldn't have listened to him," David sobbed.

"But you did," Mercy replied.

Putting his hands over his face, David cried. "Mrs. Abigail is going to skin me alive."

"Abigail has never skinned anyone alive . . . Mrs. Bell, on the other hand. . . ."

"We just wanted to try it a little bit."

"That's how the devil gets you, Dave. He just needs you to give in a little bit." Mercy frowned.

"I'll never do it again," David pleaded. "It's awful stuff, doesn't taste anything near what it smells. I thought I was a goner."

"You had me scared too," Mercy admitted. "Where's Abe?"

"Mrs. Clark recently had a baby, and seeing her husband is away on duty, Mrs. Bell asked Abe if he'd be willing to split her some firewood," David replied.

"Why didn't you go with him and help? You're right good with an axe," Mercy asked.

"Believe me, Mercy, I wish I would have."

Presently the sound of a switch meeting bare flesh mingled with agonized counting broke the silence. David flinched with each blow on his friend's bare bottom. After a short while, it stopped.

"Fourteen," Mercy said.

Soon there was the sound of dragging footsteps and muttered tones headed their way.

David braced himself. "She's coming for me!" he gasped.

When the footsteps reached their wagon, Mrs. Bell called out. "Mercy, David, I'd like a word!"

Mercy and David crawled to the buckboard where Mrs. Bell, Adelaide, and Nathaniel looked up at them.

"This is entirely my fault," Mrs. Bell began. "I don't know why men must smoke those infernal things, but it is the world we live in. Since my husband's passing, I believe I've neglected the role of discipline in my family, and my failure has led to this incident. I am sorry that it was my son who led his younger peer astray. I want you to know that he's already been punished, but if there is anything you'd like to add, he is here to receive it."

"No, I think your punishment has been fair enough. In my experience boys tend to get awfully foolish about this age, but it's usually out of love for adventure, not evil. I think David's learned his lesson, and Nathaniel too. Additional punishment isn't going to remedy them further."

Mrs. Bell nodded approvingly. "Is there anything you'd like to say?" she said, nudging Nathaniel.

"I'm really sorry, Mercy. And you too, David. I knew we shouldn't have done that, but I did it anyway. I'll never do it again . . . you had me real scared, Dave."

"I'm alright now," David assured him.

"I'll explain everything to Abigail when she gets back," Mrs. Bell said. "You needn't worry about that."

"I don't think that's necessary," Mercy piped up. "We've taken care of things here . . . I feel the matter is settled. I don't see a need to dig up a matter once it's been laid to rest, do you?"

Again Mrs. Bell nodded. "Thank you, Mercy."

Mrs. Bell turned her family around and together they walked back to their wagon, Nathaniel still rubbing his bottom the whole way.

Chapter 6

June 13, 1778

A delegation from the king, led by the Earl of Carlisle, arrived and met with our Continental Congress. Capt. Davis said the king was finally ready to come to terms, offering the colonies representation in Parliament, and a measure of autonomy. Had his offer come a year prior, the colonies may have accepted, but with French aid, and our victory over General Burgoyne, independence is finally in our grasp. Congress rightly declined the king's proposal; we've paid far too high a price to settle for anything less than liberty.

Apparently, the earl made some unsavory comments about the French, and it upset the young General Lafayette so, that he challenged the earl to a duel. Nothing came of it, however, and the meetings were conducted without incident.

The king's appeal has greatly bolstered our cause, and only made matters worse for British General Clinton. King George is no longer confident of victory, and the cost has surely grown beyond his early imaginations. Word will spread, and likely be exaggerated, of the king's misgivings and once again, both boy and man, not wanting to miss out on the opportunity to take part in the struggle, will join our ranks.

I feel there is a bit of conflict in me as I know that those who choose to join us now will no doubt receive the same accolades for their part, having never suffered the injustices born by those who fought a grim fight this past year to bring us to this point. Those who endured the hardships of 1777 will always remain the grander in my heart.

Henry says the redcoats will be abandoning Philadelphia soon, their position will not be sustainable once the French arrive. Washington has been preparing to engage them as they march for the safety of their garrison in New York. Each day we wake with anticipation of the coming conflict.

Abigail praised me highly for keeping things in order while she was away. She told me that all her anxieties had been for nothing, and apart from one incident involving a smoking pipe, the days were actually quite mundane. She seems to have come back refreshed and poured out affections on the boys as though she'd been gone for a season. I can't blame her though; the war has caused me to place a high value on every moment as well.

I thank the Lord each and every day for the opportunity to rise and serve in this place He has found for me. May He carry us all safely through the storm, and comfort those whose loved ones have paid the highest price.

Mercy Young, 15 years old.

Scouts reported on June 18th that General Clinton had at last led his army out of Philadelphia, marching to the northeast towards Sandy Hook, where the Royal Navy waited to ferry his troops to New York. On the morning of the 19th, Washington packed up Valley Forge, and the army set out to cut off the British escape.

General Lee was sent ahead with an advance party, including Henry and Benjamin's light rifle unit, to slow the British, giving the main Continental Army time to catch up. Catching the British on the road and defeating them could lead to the end of war; if they failed, the redcoats would reach New York where they had established excellent defenses and were well supplied.

This was the opportunity Washington had been waiting for; it was his turn to be the pursuer. The army moved with purpose, driven by high expectations. Countless hours of training over the long winter were now going to be tested on the field.

Mercy chose to ride with Captain Davis on a medical flatbed rather than endure the stuffy tight quarters of their wagon. The supply train consisted of hundreds of wagons that churned up dust and smelled of animal droppings. Thankfully there was a slight breeze to coax some of it off the road.

The day was hot, dreadfully hot, and before long men began dropping beside the road out of dehydration and exhaustion. Mercy and Capt. Davis collected them one by one, providing water and a little shade. Mercy worked as quickly as she could to remove the many layers they wore, some of the men were nearly cooking underneath.

By noon it was apparent the march would be met with significant casualties, and scouts reported that the redcoats, having suffered the same fate, had stopped and called it a day. Washington begrudgingly halted the march, and the soldiers made for the shade of the trees.

"Looks like we will have to march by moonlight if we want to keep this up," Capt. Davis said as he worked beside Mercy.

"Last year it was the rain, this year it's the heat," Mercy said. "We lose more boys to the weather than to redcoats. All they really need is a good swim."

"Aye, that would be the perfect cure . . . might even help with the smell." Capt. Davis smiled.

Mercy climbed from the wagon and sat in its shade, leaning back against one of the wheels. She was melting inside her dress, and though she'd had plenty to drink, she still felt faint. Closing her eyes, she did her best to ignore the swarms of flies that followed them. The march which had begun so dramatically was turning out to be a dismal affair.

Sweat rolled off her forehead, and down between her eyes, before racing to the tip of her nose and dripping to her dress below. The four layers she wore prevented the breeze from having any impact on her situation, though it helped a little when it danced across her neck. She tried to imagine herself taking a cool swim in the deep pool of the crystal-clear river near the tavern where Benjamin had fallen in trying to catch a trout.

Presently, she was shaken awake. "Mercy?" Capt. Davis said. "It's nearly a quarter to three."

Mercy winced as she opened her eyes.

"We're fixing to march again. Come on," he said, holding out his hand. Mercy took it, and he lifted her to her feet. "Everyone's rested and been given all the water they can hold. Washington is hoping the army can march until dark. We can't afford to let them slip away. The redcoats didn't lose a single man taking the Capital, we must make sure they pay a high price leaving it."

Mercy nodded, though her mind had not yet caught up with the world around her. Capt. Davis helped her up into the buckboard, orders were shouted, and the army set off again, filling the air with clouds of dust.

Mile after mile feet tromped, wheels ground, flies swirled, and sweat rolled. Though they couldn't see them, only a few miles away the British columns marched parallel with them. It was a race to the port at Sandy Hook; the discipline of both armies was being tested, and Washington wanted to prove his army was better.

Once, every hour or so, Mercy would get out of the wagon with her pail and ladle and walk amongst the soldiers, giving water to anyone who needed it. She was joined by Adelaide and many other women from the camp as they worked to keep the army on its feet. It was stifling work, amongst the ranks there was no breeze at all, and the smell of animal dung was mixed with the foul odor of sweat and poor hygiene. From time-to-time, Mercy would work her way to the edge of the column to catch a breath of fresh air before her stomach turned entirely.

"I wish the army would give these boys a double ration of soap, along with their pound of bread and beef," Adelaide groaned. "One cake of soap every two weeks doesn't seem to be cutting it."

"I'm afraid we smell little better," Mercy said. "Though, if I know Abigail, she'll have us fill the bathing barrel tonight if we're given time. A cold bath would feel heavenly after this march."

"Mmmm, good thing Henry lets the ladies go first," Adelaide said. "The water would be turned to mud after your brothers are through."

"It often is," Mercy mused.

The army marched until dark and set up camp near a stream. Tents were erected, fires stoked, and sentries posted. As Mercy had suspected, once their camp was in order, the bathing barrel was filled, and everyone took a turn. It felt heavenly to wash away the dirt and sweat of the day. Mercy always loved the way her skin felt new after a bath. Abigail nearly had to wrestle David into the barrel when his turn came.

"Mama, I already took a bath this month," David groaned from inside the sheet screen.

"Make sure you use soap, and wash that mud from behind your ears," Abigail replied dryly.

"How was the journey for you, Mama?" Mercy asked.

"Besides the fact we're moving down the road in a rolling oven, it was uneventful. The boys chose to walk most of the way, which was enough to keep them busy. Capt. Davis said there were a few boys that nearly died of the heat."

"There were, it took us a long while to get their mind to return to its rightful place. Capt. Davis said that we're going to be marching at four o'clock in the morning, resting during the hottest parts of the day, and then continuing on till dark from here on. We can't afford to show up to the battle with nearly half the army ready to faint."

"That's fine with me," Abigail sighed. "I enjoy watching the sunrise. It reminds me that every day is new, it gives me hope."

"I think I'll turn in early tonight," Mercy said. "Though my eyes enjoy a good sunrise, the rest of me isn't quite convinced of its merits."

Abigail gave her a peck on the forehead. "Goodnight, my sweet girl."

"Goodnight, Mama."

Chapter 7

They'd been marching for seven and a half days when a dispatch rider reported that General Lee had made contact with the British rear guard, inflicting nearly forty casualties, and kept up their pursuit until the redcoats took up a strong defensive position near Monmouth Courthouse. A wave of excitement tempered by anxiety washed over the ranks of Continentals. They'd finally caught up to them.

General Clinton would be forced to stop his march and defend his rear or suffer greatly before he made the port. The situation was now in Washington's hands. If he continued pursuit, there would be a battle, and if not, the British would slip away safely to New York. The full strength of both armies was about to meet on the field for the first time.

Spies reported that General Clinton was showing no signs of running, and in fact, was excited for the battle, believing his army the better. Washington had fewer numbers than the redcoats, but the French were due to arrive any day, and if he could keep his foe from escaping, they could be cut off from New York by the arrival of the French fleet and forced to surrender.

The main body of the army was a day behind the redcoats under the current circumstances. General Lee would have to engage General Clinton with his minimal light troops and keep him from escaping while the main army caught up. Henry and Ben were heading into a difficult fight.

Mercy tried to keep her mind from wandering to the dangers of her family as she carried water amongst the soldiers. She could sense the apprehension amongst the newer recruits about to be tested for the first time. If Lee was able to hold, they'd be face to face with the enemy by tomorrow afternoon.

Theo had tired of the close quarters on the road and had chosen to ride on the buckboard with Capt. Davis. Mercy nearly burst out laughing when she returned to fill her pail, only to find Theo nestled up against Capt. Davis's shoulder sound asleep. She could only imagine the awkward discomfort the young officer was feeling as he looked down on her with pleading eyes.

"You're doing grand," Mercy whispered.

Capt. Davis went to reply, but Theo's feet shifted uneasily, causing Capt. Davis to freeze.

"He's starting to warm up to you," Mercy grinned. "He usually only sleeps for a couple of hours, you'll be fine."

Capt. Davis's eyes widened.

Mercy filled her pail and walked away from the wagon, leaving Capt. Davis frozen in place.

The army marched until dark, then set up minimal accommodations for the short night. Washington would wake them early and set out for Monmouth Courthouse to relieve General Lee. Weapons maintenance was ordered, and thousands of muskets and rifles were cleaned and oiled by firelight.

Capt. Davis and Mercy prepared the medical supplies on the flatbeds; if Lee did his job, they'd show up in the middle of a fight. It'd been six months since Mercy had been near a battle, and anxiety weighed heavy in her stomach. She'd spend the short night wide awake going over the procedures she'd conducted in the past, and preparing herself for the rapid pace and grim atmosphere that awaited them.

"Have you eaten?" Capt. Davis asked.

Mercy shook her head. "My stomach is in knots; I don't think I could."

"Mine too." Capt. Davis sighed. "But you should eat something, to keep your strength up." Digging in a sack, he pulled out an apple and handed it to her.

"Thanks." Mercy smiled.

"Eat it slow. Apples are the easiest to keep down in my experience."

"I didn't think you got nervous," Mercy said.

"I'm human. I don't think we were created to grow comfortable with the suffering we heap on one another. When I was young and foolish, I couldn't wait for freedom's war to begin," he sighed, shaking his head. "Now, I long for its end with every fiber of my being."

"You're a good man," Mercy said, looking up at him. "The Lord will reward your endurance."

"And yours . . . all of you, that is," he said. "Well, I think we're as prepared as we can be at any rate. We'd best try and get some sleep."

"Yes, sir," Mercy said as he helped her down from the wagon.

"Goodnight, Mercy."

"Goodnight."

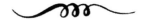

As promised, the army was up and on the march by 4 a.m. on the 27th. Dispatch riders rode back and forth between General Lee and Washington. Lee was to engage the redcoats at first light as they attempted to break camp and march out from Monmouth Courthouse.

Mercy prayed fervently for Henry and Benjamin, whose unit would be heavily outnumbered once engaged. The main army marched with purpose during the cool hours of the early morning, racing to the aid of their countrymen. Officers called out encouragement as mile after mile they closed in on their enemy.

By 8 a.m., General Lee was engaged, attacking the weakest flank of Clinton's formation, and gaining the upper hand for the moment. The temperature on the road began to climb with the sun, and the quick pace was beginning to take its toll. Mercy was nearly jogging to keep up with the ranks of men she was to water.

Sweat soaked her bonnet and saturated her dress, but she couldn't quit; Ben and Henry were out there. By 10:30 a.m., word arrived that General Clinton had reinforced his flank, and General Lee was being pushed back. A miscommunication had caused one of Lee's subordinates to extend themselves too far, putting the entire regiment at risk of folding. Lee, in turn, had called a retreat to regroup, giving Clinton time to secure better defenses, the very thing Washington had sent Lee to prevent.

The heat had grown intolerable, but Mercy could hear the battle just ahead. Distant thundering of cannons and the sharp crackle of muskets caused the ranks to stir. They were nearly there.

The army surged forward as the white smoke of battle came into view. Washington rode ahead to find Lee and gain some bearing of the battlefield, and Mercy prayed they weren't too late.

As they rounded the final bend, Washington returned and ordered the army forward at once; General Lee was about to be overrun. Officers took charge of their columns, leading them from the road and into the fight. Lee's men fell back behind Washington's and were ordered to regroup. The artillery was set, and General Knox began pulverizing the British advance.

Capt. Davis pulled the flatbed to a halt behind the artillery and ordered the other flatbeds to do the same. Mercy climbed down as several of Lee's men limped and crawled their way out of the fray. Racing to the first, she put the man's arm around her shoulder and guided him towards the flatbed. Capt. Davis pulled him aboard and together they set to work. In moments Adelaide and Abigail joined them and the flatbeds were filled. As the British continued to advance, they worked diligently in spite of the heat and conflict, forcing it from their minds.

A girl's scream cut through the din of battle. Looking up from a patient, Mercy saw a girl, not much older than herself, drop the water pail she was holding and race to the side of a fallen artilleryman. The young woman embraced his limp body for only a moment, before releasing him to lie on the ground.

In an act of true heroism, Mercy watched the girl wipe the tears from her eyes, pick up the cannonball that had fallen from the man's hands and load the cannon. Another man beside her rammed it down the barrel, the woman covered her ears, and the cannon fired. The cannon was swabbed, the powder loaded, and again she picked up a cannonball and loaded it, wiping her tears with the back of her hand between each round.

Finally, Knox's guns were able to drive the attackers back, and Washington's men were able to advance. Mercy willed herself to remain steady through constant startling cannon blasts. Every time a rifleman was added to her flatbed, she had to strangle the urge to bombard the traumatized patient with questions about Benjamin and Henry.

The battle lasted only a short while longer after Washington's army had taken the field. British General Clinton wisely retreated his soldiers back behind their stronger defensive positions. Washington, not wanting to give Clinton an advantage, also pulled back, preventing the army from being suckered into a trap. The two armies retired just out of artillery rage of one another.

Mercy's work continued in spite of the ceasefire. Oddly, many of her patients bore no wounds at all; it was the heat that had overtaken them in the field. These soldiers were laid on the ground in the shade of the flatbeds, their coats and hats removed, and water given, as much as each could hold. She was proud of them; arriving in such an exhausted state, they were still able to drive the enemy from the field and rescue General Lee's advance party, which she hoped, still included her papa and brother.

Mercy looked over to Knox's cannons. There she saw the girl, kneeling in the dirt, holding the hand of the man who'd fallen. Sunlight glistened off of tears that carved their way down powder-blackened cheeks. Mercy's heart broke for her.

Taking the water pail, Mercy made her way over to where she sat. "Here," Mercy said, holding out a full ladle. "I'm sorry for your loss."

The girl looked up at her with tired, red eyes and took the ladle, taking a long drink.

"Was he your brother?"

The girl shook her head sorrowfully. "He's—my husband."

Mercy felt pain like a dagger pierce her heart.

"We married just last year, when I turned sixteen. . . ."

Setting down her pail, Mercy knelt beside her, pulling her into an embrace. The last of the girl's resolve melted away, and she wept into Mercy's neck. In the brokenness of the moment, Mercy wept with her. All the losses they'd endured bubbled up and overflowed in the unfairness of her loss.

"I'm so sorry," Mercy whispered brokenly, running her fingers up and down her convulsing back.

Mercy held her until her tears were all used up. Members of the artillery auxiliary took her husband's body and carried it away for burial. Standing up, Mercy brushed off her dress and held out her hand; the girl took it, and Mercy lifted her wearily to her feet.

"What's your name?" the girl asked.

"Mercy, Mercy Young. What's yours?"

"Mary Hays."

"I'll stay with you, Mary Hays," Mercy said, hooking her arm.

Together they followed the gurney carrying her husband; it was laid a short way behind the American lines with six others who'd fallen during the battle. A dozen soldiers took turns digging a hole large enough to contain them all, taking breaks often for water. Mary didn't say a word, she just stared blankly at the body that'd once housed the life of her husband.

When the hole was finished, the bodies were laid carefully into it, and the reverend said a few words. A couple of the commanders spoke well of the fallen, and General Knox gave Mary his condolences. Then, one shovelful at a time, the hole was filled. That was all there was to it.

Mercy led Mary to their wagon and introduced her to Adelaide, Abigail and Mrs. Bell, and their younger siblings. Abigail told Mercy to stay with Mary, and make sure she didn't wander off alone. Adelaide was released to join them, and together they found a large tree to rest beneath.

"I saw what you did during the fight," Mercy said. "That was one of the most heroic things I've seen."

"That gun was his life. . . ." Mary replied. "I knew he'd never let it go silent so long as he had breath in his lungs. After he fell— I just knew it's what he'd want me to do."

"I'll bet he's right proud of you, looking down from glory," Adelaide said.

Mary nodded slightly.

"What will you do now?" Mercy asked.

"General Knox said I did such a fine job I'm welcome to keep it, if it's what I want."

Mercy's eyes widened.

"But you're a woman!" Adelaide said.

"He said it didn't matter to him. He said I did as fine a job as any loader in the auxiliary."

"Your husband must be proud to hear that." Mercy smiled. "Will you stay?"

"I think I need to sleep on it," Mary replied. "Everything is too fresh. My heart still expects to find him amongst the faces as they march by."

Chapter 8

On June 28th, the morning following the battle in which Mary Hays lost her husband, General Clinton's artillery bombarded the Continental positions. General Washington commanded his artillery to return in kind and the battle was on. Mercy's heart leapt when she caught sight of a dress amongst the artillerymen. There, moving through the clouds of billowing smoke and concussive blasts, was Mary, loading her gun as though it was what she'd always done.

There it was, that unbreakable American spirit. Mary fetched another ball, loaded it, cupped her ears and then reached for another ball. Her sleeves were rolled to the elbows, her hair hung wildly from her bonnet, and sweat streaked her powder-soiled face. Her movements were sharp, determined, undaunted; today the king would get a taste of a widow's wrath.

"She reminds me of you," Capt. Davis said, moving to work beside her.

Mercy blushed. "She's incredible."

"Aye," Capt. Davis replied. "That she is."

The armies bombarded each other for two hours, like roosters vying for dominion of the same barnyard. For two long hours Mary's gun never fell silent, never fell behind. Hoofbeats drew Mercy's eyes from the spectacle; it was Ben.

"General Clinton is pulling out; he's using the artillery smoke as cover. They're marching for the port; I must tell General Washington!" he said, laying his heels into the horse's flanks.

"So, that's why the bugger wasn't advancing," Capt. Davis fumed. "He wasn't softening us up, he was escaping. If they make it to New York, they'll dig in like a tick."

"He marched during the cool part of the day; it's nearly sweltering now. Our boys will not be able to pursue long in this heat," Mercy said.

Washington dispatched his cavalry and light infantry to pursue General Clinton's retreat. After a short distance, they caught up with Clinton's rear guard and gained the upper hand, forcing Clinton to abandon his escape and face the Americans once more. The battle grew fierce as the temperature soared.

Mercy and the rest of the medical staff were soon overwhelmed with patients, two thirds of which suffered from heat rather than the enemy. All available shade was strewn with soldiers on the brink of heat stroke. Mercy and Adelaide ladled water into their patients as fast as they could move, and Mercy was beginning to feel faint herself.

Nathaniel, David, and Abe raced amongst the patients, removing their wool coats, hats, and shoes. Mable and Mrs. Bell helped carry water with Mercy and Adelaide, while Abigail and Capt. Davis treated the wounded from the battle. Soldiers were slipping into shock, some vomited, others lost consciousness. Even so, Washington pressed the attack.

Mercy felt dizzy, the cracks of muskets and booms of cannons seemed dull and distant. Her world moved even when she her herself was still. She trudged on, tripping over a patient every now and again, fighting to maintain control of her wits, wanting nothing more than to pour her water pail over her fevered head.

At long last, the sun began to dip in the west. Shadows grew long, and Mercy found it easier to keep to her feet as she moved about her patients. Her head ached, along with the rest of her. Adelaide seemed to be in the same state as she stumbled about the fallen in a daze.

Finally, at nightfall, the guns went quiet. A drummer's cadence drew the army off the field, and exhausted bodies could finally find relief. A cool evening breeze danced delightfully across Mercy's damp neck, giving her momentary goosebumps.

When her pail was empty, she joined Adelaide, and together they staggered their way back to the flatbeds. When they arrived, they found Abigail sitting on a crate leaning exhaustedly back against an empty water barrel, the younger siblings lay strewn about the grass, Mrs. Bell and Capt. Davis sat on the ground against the wagon wheels.

"Good work, girls," Capt. Davis said wearily. "It's time to take a rest. The night air can tend to the boys for a bit."

Mercy nodded, nearly falling over. Taking a seat on the ground, she leaned back against Abigail's barrel, the muscles in her arms and legs quivering involuntarily as she relaxed them.

"That was a nasty one," Capt. Davis said. "We lost over three hundred today; tragically, the heat took more than the enemy. But it would have been a far worse disaster had you all not served so faithfully, though you were near to fainting yourselves. I've never seen a more dedicated display in all my life; thank you."

No one responded.

"The night will get most of these boys back on their feet, but the rest will still need care. We'll divide into shifts, I'll take the first, though I'll need an assistant."

Again, no one responded.

Mercy's body ached, and her headache had finally moved to the background; all she wanted to do was sleep for the next three days. "I'll do it," she finally said.

"Thank you," Capt. Davis sighed. "Abigail? Would you and Adelaide be willing to take the second?"

Abigail reached over and squeezed Adelaide's hand. "We'd be glad to."

"You'd best be off, then," Capt. Davis said, rising from his seat. He held out his hand and helped Abigail back onto her feet, and then Adelaide. "Make sure you take a moment to eat and get plenty of water."

"I'll see to it," Abigail replied.

"God bless you both," Capt. Davis said, sending them off.

Mrs. Bell rallied the children and led them off back to the wagons. Mercy had no doubt they'd be asleep as soon as their heads hit the pillow.

Capt. Davis fetched a pitcher of water and a tin cup. Filling it, he handed it to Mercy. "You've got the heart of a lion."

Mercy took the cup and downed the water in one go. Her weary soul had longed to follow the others into the dark, back to her bed in the wagon, but that would have meant that either her mother or friend would have to wait for the very rest she longed for, and she wouldn't have been able to rest knowing that.

Capt. Davis refilled her cup and handed it back to her.

She drank it more slowly this time, allowing herself to experience the cool liquid as it washed down her throat. Water was a conundrum, so plain, and yet, nothing had the power to refresh a weary soul like it. She loved cider, milk, and sweetened tea, but at times like these, all she longed for was water.

"Will you be alright?" Capt. Davis asked.

Mercy nodded. "I'll be stiff if I sit here much longer."

Capt. Davis held out his hand, and Mercy took it, allowing his strength to raise her. "We'll take it slow. The ones who can, need to be gotten up and moving; get them water and send them to bed. I'll send someone to bring food, a little nourishment goes a long way."

Mercy steadied herself, allowing the sudden lightheadedness to subside. "Yes, sir."

Swooping in from wherever he'd gone during the battle, Theo landed heavily on her shoulder. Mercy groaned, looking up at him; his weight felt particularly heavy after the day. Theo looked back at her expectantly, his large yellow eyes smiling at her.

"How about you carry the pail, and I'll carry the ladle," Mercy said.

Theo cocked his head sideways, blinking twice.

"Forget it," Mercy sighed, taking up the pail. "How about I do all the work and you just ride along?"

Theo blinked again.

"Yeah, I thought you'd say that."

Moving carefully amongst exhausted soldiers, Mercy tended to them gracefully in spite of her weary muscles, aching feet, and light head. She helped the ones who were able to their feet so they could return to their tents and get some sleep, the rest would need to be watered and cared for until their strength returned.

One by one her patients recovered and trudged off towards glowing fires and white tents. They'd only have the short night to rest before the battle continued in the morning. Washington had met General Clinton on the field and managed to gain the upper hand. The British were finally getting a taste of what the Continentals had endured over the past two years.

Washington intended to hold Clinton for as long as he was able in hopes that the French would arrive and cut off their retreat to New York. If Clinton's army could be captured, the war would be nearly over. It would only be a matter of time before the garrison in New York would crumble under an allied siege, and the king's army vanquished from America. Even under the grueling conditions, Washington couldn't afford to let up.

"I found us some food," Capt. Davis said, handing Mercy a bread roll. "And this is for you," he said, holding up a bit of dried fish for Theo.

Snatching the fish with his beak, Theo wolfed it down.

"Careful," Mercy said between bites. "He'll expect you to feed him from now on."

Theo stared at the doctor with his wide yellow eyes, looking him up and down.

"I see that," Capt. Davis said. "It's all I have."

"He'd probably settle for an ear," Mercy said dryly.

"Well, I'm afraid he'd have to fight me for it, I rather like them right where they are."

Mercy chuffed. "That'd be a sight to see."

"Aye," Capt. Davis mused. "I come from a long line of owl wrestlers."

Mercy snorted. "I thought your family were doctors." She teased.

"Oh, I was referring to my mother's side," he said plainly.

Mercy snorted again, and Capt. Davis burst out laughing.

Mercy smiled as he caught his breath. "You have a handsome smile," she said. "You should use it more often."

"My father used to say only fools smile all the time."

"I disagree. I think it'd take a fool not to see all there is to be grateful for. Even when things are hard, I'm still grateful to be here, for such a time as this, and it's that gratefulness that causes me to smile. If that makes me a fool . . . then I'd rather be foolish."

"I too, am grateful," Capt. Davis said. "There's nowhere I'd rather be."

Chapter 9

June 30, 1778

The battle at Monmouth Courthouse, as they are calling it, is being touted as a victory, in spite of the fact that General Clinton's army cleverly escaped last night and made their way to the port at Sandy Hook where the British navy will ferry them to New York. It is unfortunate our new allies have not shown up, they could have gallantly ended the war upon their arrival. A siege of New York will be long and costly.

I hope the poor souls we've lost since the war began can look down from Providence and see their sacrifice was not in vain. All those who doubted the cause both here and abroad have fallen silent as those who've endured the king's wrath have proved themselves able to do the thing they set out to do.

We will be moving once again to encircle the British in New York, their last stronghold in New England. The redcoats will have to devise a new strategy, as the balance of war has tipped out of their favor. Henry says we'll force them to be supplied by sea, and when the French navy is able to beat them on the water, they'll have nowhere else to go. It seems simple enough, if only the French would arrive.

Abigail has been feeling ill nearly every morning, and sometimes it lasts all day. It is a sickness that seems to come and go, and often makes it difficult for her to hold down any food. We're all worried for her; she's not got much on her to lose. Capt. Davis has often sent her to the wagon to rest and is quite perplexed himself as she shows no signs of the fever nor dysentery. Henry tries desperately to hide his worry behind his humor and optimism, I've never seen him more shaken. I'm desperate myself. I fear losing another beloved mother, and I pray fervently for God's ever-loving mercy towards her.

David has appointed himself her caregiver and rarely ever leaves her side. Abe has taken to doing both of their chores, and more, if only it will help. Mrs. Bell is also often at our wagon, giving Abigail some comforting friendship, and even Theo seems concerned for her wellbeing.

Abigail has praised us all, saying she's never felt more loved and cared for. I find the whole thing frustrating; I don't need her praise; I need her to get well. I need my mama to stay with me this time. Please God, I need her to stay.

Mercy Young, 15 years old

"She's expecting!" Capt. Davis said, emerging from the wagon. "I'm sorry, I don't know why I didn't think of it before. But I've confirmed it, she is indeed with child."

"What?!" Mercy gasped.

Capt. Davis lunged to catch Henry as he nearly fell over.

"We—we thought that was impossible. . . ." Henry said.

"After the past few years, I think I've finally come to believe that nothing is impossible," Capt. Davis said.

A strange feeling of excitement and anxiety washed over Mercy. A baby would be a grand new adventure, but it would also mean Henry and Abigail would have their own child, their own flesh and blood, and she didn't know what that would mean for the rest of them. She smiled uneasily at Henry as he ran his hand through his hair, grinning as the news sunk in.

"I'll have to temper her duties," Capt. Davis said. "Though it is good for her to be up and about, and a little work is good to keep her strong."

Henry nodded absently.

"You should be with her," Capt. Davis advised. "The news was a lot to process."

Henry took his advice and climbed into their wagon to join Abigail who was resting due to the terrible nausea she'd been experiencing. Mercy followed Capt. Davis back to the medical tent pondering a hundred imagined scenarios with growing uneasiness. A baby could change everything.

Plenty of women didn't survive childbirth. What if the baby killed Abigail? Many babies didn't survive their first year, and that would be devastating. Something like that would break Abigail's heart. What if the baby made them move back to Cambridge? What if Abigail came to love the baby more than she loved them? What if after having a child, they didn't need the Youngs anymore? They'd said that the Lord had provided them with children when they couldn't have any of their own when they first took them in. Now they did. . . .

"Mercy?"

She looked up to see Capt. Davis looking at her with a concerned expression.

"Is everything alright?" he asked.

They'd reached the medical tent, though she couldn't remember the journey. "I'm fine," Mercy said. "Just processing."

"Yes, I suppose that kind of news comes as a shock to the whole family," Capt. Davis replied.

"Yeah, family. . . ."

It was funny, she'd awoken that morning confident in who she was, that she was safe, home, even in the middle of a war, everything that mattered felt . . . sure. And now—nothing did.

"You know—"

"I said I'm fine. I best start my rounds," Mercy said, heading into the tent.

Mercy worked hard, focused, avoiding her typical banter with her patients. She did her best to steer clear of Adelaide and Capt. Davis as much as possible, not yet ready to have conversations she hadn't worked out with herself. She worked so fast to keep busy that in an hour it was becoming difficult for her to find something to do.

Collecting a small basket of soiled bandages, she carried it out of the tent towards the cauldron only to find Adelaide already stirring the pot. Her heart sank and she turned to go back into the tent.

"I'll take those," Adelaide called after her. "This is only a small batch, there's plenty of room."

Mercy turned reluctantly and carried her basket to Adelaide.

"Is everything alright?" Adelaide asked. "You've been working like we're in the middle of a battle."

"I'm fine," Mercy said.

"I heard about Abigail."

Mercy cringed. *Here it comes.*

"It's like a story from the Bible; God opening up a barren womb. She and Henry must be so excited."

"Yes, they seem to be," Mercy said, turning back towards the tent.

"Mercy?"

"What if it turns out just like the story of Abraham in the Bible?" Mercy asked, turning back. "What if Abigail and Henry get their own child and turn us out just like Sarah did to Ishmael? What if—"

She'd tried to hold it in. Tried to be stronger and have faith, but this family had come to mean everything to her. It was all she needed, all she wanted. . . .

"Oh, I could never do that, child," Abigail's voice quivered behind her.

Mercy turned to face her, and Abigail wrapped her up in her arms.

"I could never replace you, my sweet daughter. Not with a hundred babies. No one is going to take your place, not ever," Abigail said, holding Mercy's tear-streaked face in her hands. "When I dream of this new child, I see you right there with me. You've got more experience in this area than I have . . . I'm going to need your help. Knowing you'll be there with me, I'm not afraid of the challenges we'll face. Together, we'll overcome them all."

Mercy melted back into Abigail, allowing her mama to sweep her fears away. "I'm sorry," Mercy choked.

"There's nothing to be sorry for. I understand why you were frightened. To be honest, I was too when I first heard the news. But God has since given me peace, and I've decided I'm going to see the blessing for what it is. I don't rightly understand the Lord's timing, but perhaps He was simply waiting until we'd found you."

Mercy released Abigail, wiping the tears from her cheeks.

"There you go," Abigail said. "Now, will you help me raise this little one?"

Mercy nodded her head, fighting back tears that threatened to start all over again.

"That's my girl."

More than a week had passed since Capt. Davis had announced Abigail's pregnancy. Mercy and the rest of her family were on the road north to hem in the British who'd fled to New York. The last of the redcoats had set sail from Sandy Hook on July sixth, and wouldn't you know it, the long-lost French navy appeared on the eleventh. They'd missed a grand opportunity to end the war by less than three weeks. Now there was nothing left to do but battle it out.

"He did?!" David exclaimed from the back of the wagon.

"Who did what?" Mercy asked, looking up from her knitting.

"Abe heard from the postrider that a man named George Ruffles Clark attacked a fort almost by himself in Illinois," David said.

"George Rogers Clark," Abe corrected.

"What else did he say?" Mercy asked.

"Well," Abe said, situating himself. "The postrider told me a clandestine rogue, named George Rogers Clark, had tired of the British and natives raiding his townsfolk in Kentucky. So, he gathered some men, around a hundred and fifty, and then set off across the Ohio River into the Illinois territory. He said they marched for six days straight, with no food. Finally, tired and hungry, they reached the fort them raiding Philistines were coming from. It was the dead of night. Those poor boys were so awful hungry they decided to take the fort right then and there or die trying."

"And then what happened?" Adelaide asked.

"On the fourth of July, they put together a plan and rushed the fort in the darkness. To their surprise, the gates were open, and the sentries were missin' or asleep. They must not have expected an attack so far from the Continental Army. Anyway, the postrider said they took the entire fort without firing a shot! It had a funny name, Kas-Kaskaskia, that's it: Kaskaskia."

"That's incredible," Mercy said.

"That's not all," Abe said. "He's taken two more forts since then."

"When I grow up, I'm going to be just like George Rogers Clark," David said. "I'm not going to wait around for someone to tell me to do a thing, I'm just gonna go do it."

"Me too," agreed Abe. "Why, I've heard soldiers say we could have won this war three times by now if we didn't waste so much time waiting on folks to give us orders."

"We probably could have lost it three times by now as well," Abigail said, her eyes closed as she swayed with the wagon.

Abe frowned. "I suppose."

"Are we there yet?" David asked.

"Not yet," Henry said, from the buckboard.

"How much longer?" David groaned.

"Oh, not long," Henry said. "Give it another day or so."

"Another day?!" David whined. "I've spent half of my young life in the back of this wagon."

Mercy snorted, waking Theo who'd been sleeping next to Henry. Theo looked at her with annoyance, before resettling his feet and closing his eyes.

"Dave, you've got more free time to do whatever you want than the rest of us combined," Mercy whispered.

"Whatever I want?" David quipped. "Between Mama and Mrs. Bell making sure I'm healthy, safe, clean, fed, clothed, and sleepin' I hardly have a moment to myself."

Chapter 10

The army arrived in New Jersey and set up in the hills overlooking New York. It felt like Boston all over again, only this time Washington hoped the French fleet would be able to defeat the British at sea, preventing them from being resupplied. The French naval commander, Vice Admiral Charles Henri Hector d'Estaing, was continually in General Washington's tent as together they sought to come to agreement on a strategy of attack.

Almost immediately upon the Continental Army's arrival, skirmishes broke out between foraging parties which kept the medical team busy with new patients. Abigail's sickness had subsided some, and her layers were no longer able to hide the small bump growing beneath. As they settled into their new home, Mercy felt a peace she hadn't felt in years; it was only a matter of time now, they were going to be okay.

Henry and Benjamin, along with the other riflemen, were called away often to pester British redoubts, or observation points. Anything to keep the British guessing and to probe them for weaknesses. Mercy hoped that perhaps now the king would see the folly of continuing the contest, and at last let the Americans live free and give her papa back.

Mercy was nearly to the end of her rounds when Abe entered the tent.

"Oh, boy, what is it now?" she asked.

"Why do you have to ask it like that?" Abe answered in frustration. "Nothin's the matter."

"You never come to the medical tent unless somethings up," Mercy answered, putting her hands on her hips.

"She's not wrong, Abraham," Abigail agreed. "*Is* something the matter?"

"No ma'am, it's just . . . I was doing my chores, collecting and splitting wood, and I overheard some soldiers talking. They said that with the redcoats trapped in New York, the war will be over real soon, perhaps even before the year is out, and if that's true, then I'll have to live the rest of my life knowing I took no part in it."

"I pray that it's true," Abigail said. "But as for you, I'm afraid it's too late to have prevented your participation."

"Ma'am?" Abe furrowed his brow.

"You've been pulling your weight in this awful war since it began. You helped capture those redcoats in Cambridge, helped feed and sustain the army, kept them watered while they cleared Dorchester Heights, split their kindling, dug their trenches, carried our dead and wounded, captured the enemy last summer, protected your family on the road, and served faithfully. Abraham, you're every bit a soldier as any of them . . . maybe more. Surely you have born all their hardships, and your own. You don't need a uniform to be a soldier, my son, you just need the heart of one," Abigail said, brushing a bit of bark from his shoulder. "This army, and God willing, this country, are indebted to you . . . to all of you."

"Yes, ma'am," Abe smiled sheepishly.

Abigail planted a peck on his cheek. "Now go, keep up the good work. This war may very well be near its end, but it is not over."

"Yes, ma'am," Abe said, giving her a final squeeze before ducking out the flap.

"You're the best mama I've ever seen," Mercy said.

As Abigail turned, Mercy noticed tears in her eyes.

"What is it?" Mercy asked.

Abigail shook her head, biting her lip. "I'm sorry, Mercy, my emotions have been getting the better of me since I heard I was pregnant. For years I dreamed one day I'd have a child, and then

I surrendered that dream when no child came, and now . . . my life is so full, so very full, and when you say things like that I feel as though I'm living in a dream . . . this couldn't be my life. I'm not meant to have any children, to hear their laughter at Christmas, or wipe their frightened tears after a bad dream, or hear them call me mama. . . ."

Mercy stepped forward and caught Abigail in her arms. She'd gotten this way a few times in the past and it seemed best to let her work through it.

"How is it that I have become so blessed to be called the best mama? I can scarce make myself believe it."

"This little one couldn't be born to a better woman," Mercy said. "It'll be the envy of all the other young one's not near so fortunate."

"Don't overdo it," Abigail blushed. "The Good Lord has everyone well in hand."

"Yes, ma'am."

Abigail took a deep breath, letting it out slowly. "Let's finish here and then go find some sauerkraut."

"Some what?! Yuk!" Mercy gagged.

"I don't know what it is, but for the last week I've been craving nothing else. Sauerkraut and fish," Abigail said.

Mercy held her stomach, pretending to vomit.

"Do you want this little one to go hungry?" Abigail pleaded.

"Fine," Mercy sighed. "You find the sauerkraut, and I'll catch you some fish, but I am not eating that—I'd rather starve."

"Best take the boys—I'm craving lots of fish."

That afternoon Mercy and Adelaide, along with their siblings set out for the clear streams in the valley below their camp. Theo noticed the fishing canes and glided from his perch on the buckboard to Mercy's shoulder where he danced in anticipation.

"I'm glad we sleep under the wagon," David said. "Mama's been eating pickles, onions, and sauerkraut like they're sugar candy, and puts vinegar on everything. If she keeps it up, that baby is liable to come out awful bitter."

"I had to hold my breath the last time she gave me a good talking to," Abe said. "My eyes were watering."

"Our mama liked pickled things when she was pregnant with Mable," Adelaide said.

"Maybe that means she's going to have a girl?" Mercy suggested.

"Sounds right," Abe agreed. "Girls are more bitter than boys."

"As if!" Mercy hissed.

"Sec!" Abe said, flinching under her gaze.

"Well, if we are," Mercy began. "It's because arrogant little boys have driven us to it!"

"I'm not arrogant," David said. "I know boys are better than girls . . . but I don't make a big deal about it, right Nathaniel?"

Nathaniel looked over at his sister and Mercy wide eyed.

"We talk about it some, but not in front of girls so they don't feel bad," David continued. "That's the humble way to do it."

Suddenly, Mercy forgot all about fishing as she strangled the cane pole in her hand.

"Haha, Dave. We should probably stop talking and start fishing," Abe chuckled nervously, giving his brother a gentle push towards the water.

Mercy glared at them as they passed in front of her.

"Boys," Adelaide chuffed. "The only critter in all of God's creation too daft to realize God had to make a whole other creature because He saw they were helpless on their own. . . ."

Mercy snorted. "Except Ben?"

"No," Adelaide sighed. "He's so utterly helpless it's adorable. He can hardly buckle his shoes if I so much as smile at him."

"He's becoming a fine man," Mercy said. "I'm proud of him."

"He is," Adelaide agreed.

"Do you think there's any hope for these three?"

"Mama says it's one of God's mysteries, but somehow, they all seem to make it sooner or later," Adelaide said.

"Here, Mercy, let me bait your hook for you," Abe said, taking Mercy's cane.

"What about Adelaide's?" Mercy asked.

"I'll get it," Nathaniel piped up.

Mercy smiled on the inside. It seemed the boys were feeling a bit repentant, though it'd be best to let them think on it for a good long while.

"All set," Abe said.

"Thank you," Mercy said airily, taking her cane and flicking her line out into the stream.

It was another hot and humid day, and in a short time the girls found themselves sitting on a log the boys had rolled to the water's edge for them, dipping their toes into the cool water like queens.

"This feels heavenly," Adelaide said, closing her eyes.

"Got one!" Mable called, fighting a moderately-sized trout to shore.

"I've got one too!" David said, dragging his own fish ashore.

"That's one to one," Adelaide said.

And the Bell vs. Young tournament had begun.

Mercy caught the next one, and then Abe. Next Mable and Adelaide each caught one, and things were all tied up. Nathaniel hooked up with a larger brown striped fish, with pretty bronze eyes, which put up a grand fight until he was able to horse it to shore.

Then Mable hooked another large fish which got her line tangled up in some sticks under the water. Abe pulled off his shoes and stockings, shrugged off his shirt, and dove in after her line. He was under the water for a considerable moment before he came to the surface, clinging tightly to a large trout.

"Thank you, Abe," Mable smiled.

"Ah, it was nothing. I was looking for an excuse to go for a swim anyway."

"That puts the Bells up by two," Adelaide said.

"Come on, boys!" Mercy cheered. "Keep after 'em."

"But Abe done churned up all the water," David complained.

"Just give it a minute, Dave. It'll be right in no time," Abe said.

By the end of the day, the Bells won the contest nine to six, and also caught the two largest fish of the day. It was a rare yet humbling defeat for the Youngs.

Adelaide and Mercy led their little column of adventurers as they hiked back to camp; the boys reeked of fish, worms, and sweat. Everything felt good and right, even optimistic. A year ago, they were battling nearly constant torrential rains, agonizing defeats, and starvation. Men were rotting in their uniforms while they marched, and now . . . the sun was shining, the redcoats were encircled in New York, and the army was being supplied by the French. The difference was surreal.

When they arrived back at the wagons, Abigail nearly pounced on them with excitement, and Mercy could smell she'd already found her sauerkraut. Abe cleaned and gutted the fish and set them to roast over the fire. Theo organized the pile of fish remains with all the care of an aristocrat, determining which morsels he'd savor first. Mercy fetched some water and prepared it for coffee.

"So, tell me about your adventure," Abigail said, pulling David to sit beside her.

"The Bells won," David mumbled.

"Well, certainly there must be more to the story than that."

"There's nothing worse in the whole world than losing to Nathaniel Bell," David groaned.

"Oh, it can't be that bad," Abigail chided. "You Youngs win most of the time, as I hear it."

"We do," David agreed. "But when we lose . . . Nathaniel won't let me hear the end of it for a week. It makes me so mad; I just want to hit him in the nose."

"Good gracious!" Abigail chuffed. "And would that change the outcome of the fishing contest?"

"No, ma'am," David frowned. "But it sure would make me feel good."

"Don't you think that would have a negative impact on your friendship?" Abigail asked.

"That, and he's likely to whoop you," Abe said. "He's nearly as old as I am, and a bit bigger."

"Perhaps it'd be better to take the high road," Abigail suggested. "Allow him a little gloating, and then beat him soundly the next time you have a contest."

"And then I'll get to do the gloating?!" David asked excitedly.

"I've always found the best gloating to be no gloating at all," Abigail said. "It shows that winning is common to you, expected, nothing to get excited about."

"But you *are* excited, aren't you?" David asked.

"Of course! But my opponents don't need to know that."

David smiled. "Alright, Mama, I'll do it your way."

Chapter 11

W e'll be marching out under General Greene," Henry said. "Generals Lafayette and Sullivan will be going too. The French navy will keep the British navy at bay and deliver French troops ashore for the assault."

"Why Rhode Island?" Abigail asked.

"I suspect there are a few reasons," Henry said. "It would tighten the noose on those garrisoned in New York. There's a significant force there which, if captured, would be a serious blow to the enemy. This would also allow us to take a test run at a coordinated attack using both French and American elements. It'll probably take a few battles before we all learn to work well together."

"How long?" Abigail asked.

"A month at the least," Henry replied. "I'm sorry, my love."

Abigail inhaled deeply, slowly letting it out. "We'll be alright. The sooner you boys end the war, the sooner we can all go home."

"That's right," Henry said, leaning over and planting a kiss on the top of her head.

"When are you leaving?" David asked.

"They want us ready to march by 4 a.m. so we can make good time before the sun gets high," Benjamin replied.

"It's nearly August," Abigail sighed. "Another month and the heat should be behind us."

"Aye," Henry replied.

"You'd best go spend a moment with Adelaide before it gets too dark," Abigail suggested to Ben. "Lord knows she can hardly eat when you're away."

"Yes, Mama," he said, bowing respectfully before dashing off towards the Bell's wagon.

"I think the boys and I should turn in," Mercy said. "There's going to be plenty to do in the morning."

"No there ain't!" David scoffed.

"Come on, Dave," Abe said, taking him by the arm.

Mercy gave Henry a hug, and Abigail a peck on the cheek before leaving them alone beside the fire.

"Why are we going to bed now?" David asked, twisting to free his arm as they reached the wagon.

"Because Mama and Papa needed a moment alone," Mercy said, nodding her thanks to Abe.

"Why? I'm gonna miss them just as much, maybe more," David retorted.

"It's a different kind of missing," Mercy said. "A deeper kind, something only felt by two people who love each other the way they do." She nodded towards the silhouettes leaning on one another silently in the firelight.

David glanced towards the fire, and for the first time, he had nothing to say.

"It's that love that keeps us all safe. It makes room for all of us," Mercy said, ruffling his hair.

"I *am* going to miss them," David said at last.

"We all are, buddy," Abe agreed.

David nodded, climbing into his hammock.

Mercy lit a candle and lay down with her diary. Her emotions were flustered and frustrated at the position they found themselves in. The war had clearly taken a turn, even the king's men sensed it, and yet her papa and brother would be marching out again. There would be battles and boys would fall, maybe even them, in a contest that seemed to be all but concluded. What a waste those losses would be, just because the king wasn't quite ready to say uncle yet.

If she ever laid eyes on the king, it'd take an army to keep her from slapping the crown right off his head. Mercy determined there should be a law stating every governing official should have to be a military physician prior to taking office, so the cost of their wars would be fully understood by those who'd send men to die in their stead. Empires were not built by emperors but by the blood and broken lives of common men and women.

Mercy knew Henry and Abigail would sit by the fire long into the night in spite of the early morning. Abigail would hold him tightly, listening to the beats of his heart and the soft sounds of his breath. She'd hold him, like it could be her last time, she'd hold him without regret. And in the early grays of morning, she'd hold him one last time, and he'd disappear into the darkness, called away by the soft cadence of the drummer boy.

These were the souls who'd bear the birth pains of a new nation, the ones on whom the history books would fail to bestow rightful glory, their sacrifices overshadowed by those who wore embellished uniforms and fancied themselves the grander. Romantic folks, too quick to forget that a general is nothing without his army, just as a king ought not to forget that apart from his people, he rules nothing.

Tyranny crumbles when the common people rise against it.

Mercy awoke the following morning beside a spent candle. She'd fallen asleep while writing, leaving a long smudge across the page. Fortunately, this time, her face had not landed on the fresh ink, and she had not awoken to her words mirrored on her cheek, an event the boys had found most amusing.

The sun was already rising, Henry and Ben were already on the march. She rose and stretched; the awkward position she'd spent the night in left her neck stiff and sore. Emerging from the wagon, she found a weary, red-eyed Abigail working the fire for breakfast.

"Good morning, dear," Abigail said, forcing a smile.

"Morning, Mama," Mercy said, giving her a peck on the cheek.

"They've gone," Abigail said.

"I know," Mercy replied softly.

"You'd think I'd be used to it by now. . . ."

"I don't see how a person could. I know I'll feel an emptiness until they return. Even if I keep busy every moment."

Abigail nodded.

"I'll fetch some water for coffee," Mercy said.

"You'd best make it strong," Abigail sighed. "I haven't slept a wink."

Mercy loved the smell of coffee, and she wished it tasted like it smelled, though she'd learned that adding a bit of milk or cream seemed to do the trick. On mornings like this one, she knew

Abigail would drink it strong and black, allowing the bitterness to awaken her senses. She hoped the baby wouldn't have to endure the same awful taste. She'd asked Capt. Davis how a baby ate in the womb, and he'd said there was a special cord that fed directly into the baby's stomach, so perhaps the flavor would be avoided entirely.

She met Adelaide at the water barrel fetching water for the Bells. Adelaide looked in as poor a condition as Abigail.

"You look terrible," Mercy said.

"Thanks," Adelaide groaned.

"Did you sleep at all?"

"Only a bit. We stayed up most the night near the fire talking."

"About what?"

Adelaide blushed. "You know, how long he was going to be gone, and missing each other, and . . . marriage."

Mercy almost dropped her pail.

"What?" Adelaide grinned. "Folks are saying the war is almost over."

"Yeah, but—"

"Mary Hays was married at sixteen, remember? I'll be seventeen in February. . . ."

"Yeah, but—"

Adelaide snorted. "Don't swallow your tongue, Mercy. We were just talking and dreaming, there's no date set or anything. Ben hasn't even sought Jonathan's blessing yet. It just gives us hope, you know, to look ahead and see something on the other side of all this. It's something to fight for."

Mercy nodded. "Sorry, it's my hope too; just caught me off guard is all."

Adelaide smiled, hooking Mercy's free arm, and together they walked back to the wagons.

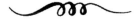

Later that morning, at the medical tent, Mercy performed her duties with care, flinching every now and again as soldiers on either side of the conflict caught sight of the other. Most of the shooting of that kind was harmless, and it was luck, more than skill, which caused a musket ball to find its mark. Still, it was enough to prevent anyone from truly relaxing, leaving the muscles tight and exhausted at the end of each day.

Capt. Davis moved about the tent from patient to patient with a maddening indifference. He seemed not to notice the shots at all, nor to fret himself over the fact that half the army was off to Rhode Island without them. His only care seemed to be what was right in front of him as he mused over a ruptured boil or a new infestation of scabies, scribbling notes in his book with apparent rapture at each new puzzle.

He'd surely tell her that to worry about either was a waste of both time and effort, as worry would do nothing to change them. Which she already knew was maddeningly true. Then he'd tell her to focus on what was in front of her, which was the usual host of disgusting consequences of poor hygiene or parasite infestation. How could any sane person want to focus on that?

Her current patient was suffering from a bad case of scabies, a common ailment amongst the ranks of soldiers. It was a parasite that burrowed under the skin and reproduced, leaving a swath of itchy festering bumps. If the infestation grew bad enough, an infection would develop, and a man could die. Mercy gently spread turpentine over the infected area, and her patient grunted as the thick ointment burned his sensitive skin.

"You'll need to bathe as often as you're able, and change your uniform when it's soiled, and apply more turpentine until they're gone," Mercy said.

"But it's all the clothing I have. We haven't been given new uniforms in a year," the man said.

"If I had a way, I'd get you another pair of breeches at the least, but—" Mercy started.

"I heard just yesterday that a French ship has arrived," Capt. Davis cut in, "bringing new supplies and uniforms; they'll be distributed shortly. Until you receive yours, I've got an extra pair of breeches here you can have. Wash your uniform at night and hang it to dry by the fire, it'll be ready by morning."

"Thank you, sir," the man said humbly, bowing to Capt. Davis.

"Thank you for your faithful service, Jonathan," Capt. Davis bowed in return, and the man started back to camp.

"That was good of you," Mercy said.

"I'm tired of losing patients to a lack of proper laundry," Capt. Davis replied dryly.

"Are there really French supplies coming?"

"Aye. Some have already found their way to camp, but it'll take a few days to distribute them," Capt. Davis said, taking a sip of coffee.

"That's good, I was afraid you were going to run out of breeches since we have several more patients with scabies, and you've nobly taken it upon yourself to clothe them."

Capt. Davis coughed, spitting some of his coffee into the air. He glanced around the room, nervously processing the number of soldiers looking back at him expectantly.

"It's almost a shame that ship arrived," Mercy said. "Instead of giving the shirt off your back, you were willing to give the breeches off your legs. It would have been biblically heroic."

Capt. Davis choked on his coffee again, sending him into a coughing fit.

"The boys *were* looking a mite haggard coming out of Valley Forge," Mercy continued, pretending not to notice. "It'll be nice to see them all looking smart in new uniforms."

"Aye, it's a good thing the ship has arrived," Capt. Davis said, clearing his throat. "A sharp looking uniform has a profound impact on a soldier. Makes him feel his worth and gives him a sense of honor."

"Then these men deserve it," Mercy said.

"Aye," Capt. Davis agreed.

"Will that be no breeches for us then?" asked one of the soldiers waiting to be seen.

Mercy watched Capt. Davis cringe, before putting on a pleasant smile and turning to face them. "Let me see how many more I have at my disposal," he said, walking briskly into his quarters.

Mercy turned away to stifle a laugh, before moving on to the next patient.

Capt. Davis was about to give away his last spare pair of breeches when the soldiers were called to gather by company to receive their new uniforms.

"You really are a hero," Mercy said as they watched the spectacle from the tent flap.

"If only I'd waited a day," he sighed.

"But then I wouldn't have gotten to see it, and that would've been a shame," Mercy said.

"I'm glad I could provide you some amusement," Capt. Davis chuffed.

"I wasn't amused," Mercy said. "Well, maybe a little, but mostly, I was proud of you."

Capt. Davis straightened. "Still, I'm afraid I must now fall upon the mercy of the quartermaster. A surgeon needs several pairs of breeches; our work is a messy one."

Chapter 12

A man named Barron Von Steuben had joined their camp during the winter. He had a thick Prussian accent and carried himself with great discipline. Washington, noting Steuben's extensive military service in past wars, put him in charge of training the army. Over the past several months he had put together a model company of soldiers who were able to move with discipline under fire, use the bayonet, which previously hadn't been used by the Continental Army, and respond effectively to commands regardless of the terrors of the battlefield.

This company and its officers were then assigned the task of training all of Washington's army. The drilling was intense, and Mercy witnessed firsthand the improvements to discipline both on and off the field. Morale improved, decorum improved, and even hygiene improved. As a direct result, the numbers of patients began to fall, as soldiers were required to keep themselves in good presentation order.

"They march as fine as the redcoats," Abigail said as they watched a company drilling on the parade field.

"It may have something to do with General Von Steuben putting such harsh consequences on soldiers being drunk on duty," Adelaide said. "It's awful hot out to find yourself standing in the stocks."

"Men do seem to march straighter when they can see straight," Mercy agreed.

"Oh, it's more than that, girls. Look at them, there's a bit of pride in that step. He's helped them believe in who they are. The king has treated us as peasants for so long, men begin to forget that they're men. But that Von Steuben, he's found a way to remind them of who they are. A man who knows who he is, well . . . Jesus was such a man."

"The Lord Jesus didn't fight . . ." Mercy replied skeptically.

"Didn't he?" Abigail replied. "Then how come when He confronted the pharisees with His teaching did those around Him say, who is this man? No one ever taught the way that He does. Or when the devil himself tempted Him in the wilderness and questioned *if* He was the Son of God, did He not stand His ground? And when he went as a lamb to that awful cross, was it not for us that He laid down his life? And on the third day, with all hell standing guard, did He not rise from the dead, conquering sin and death?! Sounds like quite the warrior to me."

"I guess his fight was a different kind," Adelaide said. "Not fought against flesh and blood, or with weapons of wood and iron."

"And it's still being fought today in a million human hearts," Abigail said.

"Didn't Jesus say to love our enemies as we love ourselves?" Mercy asked.

"That He did," Abigail said.

"Then are we wrong for fighting this war?" Mercy asked.

"He didn't say they weren't our enemies, only that we should treat them the same way we'd treat our own. And in that tent over there we do our best. If they're hungry, we feed them; if they're thirsty, we give them something to drink; if they're wounded, we care for them," Abigail said.

"Do you think they're treating my papa the same way?"

"I don't know, dear," Abigail said, wrapping an arm around her. "Henry has sent letters seeking news to London, but he's heard nothing. The Lord only knows if his requests even arrive."

"I didn't know he was looking for my papa," Mercy said in surprise.

"He loves you, Mercy. And you love your papa. Of course, he'd try and find him," Abigail said. "He didn't tell you because he didn't want to get your hopes up, but he's been awaiting a reply as anxiously as you would."

"The king won't be very obliging to those he deems started the conflict," Mercy sighed. "I'd be a fool to get my hopes up."

"Not a fool," Abigail said. "A good daughter."

"When our work gets slow, like it is now, I find my mind running to all sorts of cruel fantasies regarding the ones I love," Mercy said.

"Mine too," Adelaide agreed.

"Why don't you girls give Mrs. Bell a break and take your siblings on an adventure?" Abigail suggested. "Find some water to splash in; it'd feel lovely on a day like today."

"Alright," Mercy agreed.

"Best bring a cane . . . the little one is craving fish again." Abigail smiled.

"Theo would probably be disappointed in me if I didn't," Mercy said.

The girls collected their siblings from Mrs. Bell, who gratefully called the school day early, and made their way down to the steam in the valley behind their camp. Immediately, the boys set to work hunting crayfish and frogs, while the older girls sat on a log dipping their feet in the cool water. Mable found a deep pool a short distance upstream to try her hand at fishing.

"I heard one of the Frenchmen say that the French eat frog legs," Nathaniel said.

"Eww," Adelaide gaged.

"I'd be willing to try it," Abe said. "The big green frogs have some pretty thick legs."

"Let's catch a few and try them," Nathaniel agreed.

Mercy watched with amusement as the boys dove this way and that to grab a frog only to have it squirt through their fingers.

"What are you going to carry them in?" Adelaide asked.

"I don't know . . . I'll roll up the bottom of my shirt like a basket and carry 'em in that," Nathaniel said.

"Mama's going to have a fit," Adelaide said, shaking her head.

"Look at this monster!" David said, holding up a massive bullfrog that was wider than his palm.

Theo danced on Mercy's shoulder, preparing to take off.

"NO, THEO!" David shouted. "This is MY frog!"

Theo steadied his feet, looking to Mercy dejected.

"I've got something!" Mable called. "It's not very big, but it's putting up a fight." Lifting her line from the water, she jumped back as an odd creature swung at her. "What on earth!" Mable gasped.

"What is it?" Abe called.

Mable lifted her line. "It's the biggest crayfish I've ever seen!"

Unable to bear the anticipation, Theo blasted from Mercy's shoulder straight for Mable.

Screaming, Mable dropped her cane on the grass, darting out of his way. The miniature lobster hit the ground, letting go of her worm and righting itself just as Theo skidded to a halt in front of it. The creature tucked its tail and raised its claws into the air snapping wildly. Theo, a little perplexed that Mable had not caught a helpless fish as he had supposed, pranced around his prey, desperate to find an advantage.

After several moments of frustration, Theo decided his superior size was enough and went straight at the crafty critter. Surprisingly, the crayfish didn't make a run for it, instead it snapped its large claws in Theo's face, causing the confused bird to jump back in surprise.

In frustration, Theo tried stomping at the creature, who again, went on the offensive, and Theo was forced to retreat. Not one to be outdone by a slimy water bug, Theo attempted to hurdle the critter and attack it from the rear. The plan probably would have worked, had the crayfish not taken a desperate swipe and latched onto Theo's tail feathers.

A chorus of laughter erupted as Theo spun this way and that, trying to dislodge his attacker. He rolled on his back kicking and flopping, but the crayfish held fast. In a last, desperate attempt to free himself, Theo took flight. He rose awkwardly over the water finally scoring a desperate kick to his opponent, dislodging one of his tailfeathers, allowing his foe to float gracefully to the water, and sink below the surface still clutching Theo's feather.

Theo circled the ripples twice, before returning to Mercy's shoulder in humiliation.

"Awe, it's okay, boy," Mercy said, stroking Theo's chin, as he looked away in embarrassment. "He just wanted it more than you did today."

"I'll say," David laughed. "That was the funniest thing I've ever seen!"

"Agreed," Nathaniel said. "Theo was fighting for his life!"

Mercy felt bad for her little friend, but the spectacle had brought her to tears, and her ribs still felt the ache. The feisty little critter reminded her of the Americans taking on the majestic British Army. Ugly, and out of its element, it had chosen to fight its superior oppressor. Had it given up, Theo would have eaten it for sure, but its tenacity had saved its life and won its freedom.

"Are you alright, Mable?" Mercy called.

Mable returned to her cane, and after checking her worm, tossed the line back into the stream. "I'm fine, I was only startled. Theo can look right terrifying when he's coming straight at you like that."

"He doesn't look very terrifying right now," David balked.

"That's enough, Dave!" Mercy snapped. "Can't you see he's already humiliated enough? What good does it do to continue to bully him?!"

David stopped smiling and looked at his toes. "Sorry, Mercy. I didn't mean to be a bully."

"Why don't you try and see if you can catch him a fish. That'll probably help him to forget all about it," Mercy said.

In the end it was Mable who caught a small fish, and after some coaxing, Theo flew over to cautiously investigate, before swallowing it whole. The boys had caught a substantial number of frogs that writhed inside the fabric of Nathaniel and Abe's shirts. Mercy couldn't wait to hear what Mrs. Bell and Abigail had to say about their little frog feast idea.

"Absolutely not!" Mrs. Bell said, as the boys explained their idea. "And you'll be washing your own shirt, Nathaniel Bell!"

Mercy felt for Nathaniel as he hung his head in disappointment. The morning had been filled with so much excitement and anticipation, the kind that seems to fill young adventurous boys who believe there is no such thing as a bad idea.

"Hey, she didn't say we couldn't ask Abigail," Abe whispered as they walked away, their shirts still churning with frogs.

They found Abigail in the medical tent, and the boys laid out their idea.

"You say the French eat them?" Abigail asked skeptically.

"Aye, they do," Capt. Davis said, who'd found himself drawn to their amusing conversation. "They consider them a delicacy. I'd be inclined to try them myself."

"You hear that, Mama? A delicacy," Abe said.

Abigail's face contorted a little as Mercy watched her opposition fade.

"Alright," Abigail sighed. "You do the work of cleaning them, and you," she said, pointing to Capt. Davis. "You're joining us for dinner."

"It'd be my pleasure, ma'am," Capt. Davis said, bowing.

The boys looked at each other, eyes wide with excitement, before bounding out the flap.

"Oh, Mercy . . . what have I done?" Abigail said.

"I think we'll know come dinner," Mercy replied, swallowing hard.

"I haven't the faintest idea how to cook frog," Abigail groaned.

"They're kinda like fish; why not just bread them with flour and salt?" Mercy asked.

"That does seem like the most sensible thing. . . . This is Mr. Hadley's doing. He's turned all my children feral."

"I'll help you fry them," Mercy said, taking Abigail's hand. "It may actually taste good."

"Lord, let it be," Abigail prayed, looking to the sky.

That evening the delicious smell of fried frog legs wafted through the wagon. The boys had first brought the legs skinned, but with the feet still attached. Poor Abigail's weakened stomach had her running for the tall weeds at the edge of the camp. A short while later the boys had returned with the legs, feet removed, and now they looked much like squirrel's legs.

Abigail was able to regain her constitution, and together she and Mercy battered and fried the nearly forty legs. Capt. Davis said grace, and everyone watched in trepidation as the young captain took the first bite. He chewed slowly, contemplatively, and then swallowed.

"Well?" Abigail asked.

He dabbed the corners of his mouth with a handkerchief. "That . . . was *fantastic* eating!" He smiled.

Abe dove in, taking a large bite of one of his legs, he chewed it twice. "Mm-mmm, this *is* good!" he declared, his mouth still full.

Mercy watched Abigail whisper a prayer to the heavens before taking a small bite. A soft smile pulled at the corners of her mouth. "Mercy," she gasped. "It's actually delicious! Bless the Lord!"

With that, everyone set in. Abigail sent David to fetch the Bells, and after some coaxing on Abigail's part, Mrs. Bell took a bite . . . and then another, and another. Though it clearly pained her to admit, she'd been wrong about the frogs. When they'd finished, there wasn't a leg left over, and Mercy knew that frog legs would be joining the already odd assortment of table fare keeping them alive in the camp.

Chapter 13

August 17, 1778

The horrible storm which has assailed us for the past couple of days appears to have worn itself out and has finally passed on. There is debris and mud everywhere, reminding me of the bitter struggles of the past year. The wind was so violent the canvas on our wagon pulled free and will need mending. Much of our belongings were saturated before we could resecure the canvas; even as I write, I must contend sadly with the warped pages of my diary.

Still, as Abigail would say, we are all in one piece. I pray the sun shines in the morning; there is no lack of items that will need to be hung out to dry. I loathe trying to sleep when everything is damp and sticky, and the pungent smells that have lain dormant in our tiny home have awoken.

Abigail is suffering worse than I, tossing and turning, stopping only to stifle a gag. She got up and went to the medical tent a short while ago, I think she aims to spend the night there on a dry cot. The boys, however, seem to sleep like the dead no matter what their condition, and I must say I envy them for that.

Before the storm, we'd received word that the Americans sieging Rhode Island had secured their positions, and that the French navy had defeated a small British fleet and had begun deploying French troops to encircle the redcoats and capture Newport. Everything seems to be going according to plan.

Capt. Davis says if the French navy is able to defeat the redcoats at sea, the redcoats in Rhode Island will be cut off from supply and won't be able to hold out for long. It sounds as though the siege is nearly over, but then he says in his dry Capt. Davis way, "But alas, the British possess the premier naval force in the world, the French are sure to have their hands full." And then he takes a sip of his coffee as though it is neither here nor there. He is both the most charming and infuriating man I've ever met.

To listen to him, you'd believe the war will go on forever and that there's no higher calling than to live out our days fulfilling our duty in that glorified butcher's shop. Not that I would complain about my work, I do feel blessed to give care and a bit of peace or even joy to those serving the cause, but for pity's sake, does he have to be so bleak? To make matters worse . . . he's usually right, and even that fact he seems to regard with indifference.

Deep down, I sense he's gloating over the fact his dreary predictions so often prove more accurate than my optimistic musings, though I've no proof other than my own sour dissatisfaction at his apparent nonchalance. I can only assume he's taking the high road, making him all the more infuriating and subliminally arrogant. A real gentleman would . . . would gloat, just a little, so that I was aware that they were aware they'd defeated me, and then profusely apologize for having wounded my pride. Yes, that is what a true gentleman would do.

Well, when the French navy defeats the British in the upcoming battle, I'll have to show him how it ought to be done. Surely a merciful God wouldn't deny me this one small victory.

Mercy Young, 15 years old

The following morning, after a lean breakfast, Mercy and Adelaide tiptoed their way across the soggy ground to the medical tent. The storm had ushered in a welcomed cool breeze, and here and there soldiers sat contentedly around smokey fires sipping coffee and murmuring quietly. Capt. Davis sat outside the tent on a stump poking at the coals in the fire ring as he sipped his own mug.

"Good morning," he nodded.

"Good morning, sir," the girls replied.

"Have you heard the latest reports?" Capt. Davis said.

"No, sir," Mercy replied.

"A dispatch rider arrived early this morning. Unfortunately, the French fleet has taken a terrible beating during the storm and has retrieved their troops and set sail to Boston for repairs, leaving the Americans to conduct the siege alone. As you can imagine, General Sullivan was not at all pleased, and I'm afraid his words have cast our allies in a poor light. Sullivan claims the siege was only days from success, and without the French, it will be difficult to succeed," Capt. Davis said.

Mercy kicked the water pail at her feet sending it bouncing across the ground end over end, flinging water everywhere. Pain shot through her toes, but she clenched her jaw to hide it. *Why? Why couldn't they just win?!*

"Are you alright, Mercy?" Capt. Davis asked. "I didn't mean to upset you. I know your father and brother are there."

"Looks like you were right again, sir!" Mercy said, through clenched teeth. Throwing open the flap, she limped inside the tent.

Working through her responsibilities like a storm, Mercy moved from patient to patient changing bandages, providing water, and treating parasites absent her normal charm. Sweat rolled down her cheeks as she worked feverishly to avoid contact with Capt. Davis. Maybe he was right, maybe the stupid war would go on forever, or at least until there were no men left to fight it. Maybe she'd just let herself become gloomy like Capt. Davis; the price of optimism was far too painful.

Her foot hurt too, with every step it reminded her of her outburst, louder and louder, until she felt its ache throughout her whole body. She reddened with the futility of it all as hot tears trembled near the edge of her eyes. It was all so foolish. Kicking the bucket was foolish, she was foolish, the war was foolish. . . .

The pain and frustration were dizzying; the world around her began to churn, and then . . . hands. Strong, gentle hands caught her arms and halted her spinning world.

"Mercy," Capt. Davis said. "I'm sorry. I am sure I have in some way disappointed you, and you are probably right for thinking so. I don't know what it is, but I regret it ardently, and ask your forgiveness before you harm yourself on my account."

She wanted to pull away, to stay angry and foolish, but her foot ached, and his words were sincere, and his eyes pleaded with her heart in honest pity. Relaxing, she allowed herself to be led to an empty cot where he carefully sat her down.

"Will you permit me to look at your foot?"

Mercy nodded, and a fresh wave of pain and heat washed over her as he slipped off her shoe.

"It's badly swollen." He frowned. "I can see that without even removing your stocking." Slowly he began to slip her stocking painfully over her toes.

"Why do you have to be right all the time?!" Mercy grunted.

Capt. Davis didn't answer as he laid her stocking beside her on the cot.

"Every time I feel there's hope that this war could end, you always have to say something like, 'The redcoats have the best navy in the world so . . .' and then we lose," Mercy whimpered. "And I look like a fool for being hopeful, because you're always right, and it's never going to end."

"I never said it isn't going to end," Capt. Davis said, probing her big toe.

"Why can't you just be hopeful?"

"Is that what you want to hear, even though in my heart I know that the likelihood is not promising?"

"Argh! See! How could you have been so sure that it couldn't have been the end?"

"Because I'm a realist . . . I look at the facts, what I know about our army and theirs. I've never said they are unbeatable, only that they will not be beaten so easily."

"Is it wrong for me to hope they'll be beaten quickly?"

Capt. Davis paused his probing. "Mercy, it isn't that I don't hope for that, I just don't hang my emotions on it. I can hope for one, while accepting the other, and carry on with my part either way. Otherwise, I could do great harm to my patients, or even myself, as you did today."

Mercy cringed as a new pain shot through her.

"Those boys in there need you, Mercy. And this morning they didn't get you, they got something else. The battlefield is filled with enough anger and frustration; our job is to administer peace, not a storm. Perhaps I temper your hopes not to be right or wrong, but so that you, while possessing the one, may be able to endure the other."

Mercy let her tears fall. "I'm tired of enduring. . . ."

"I know . . ." he sighed. "I am too."

She closed her eyes.

"You're the strongest person I know, Mercy, and I'm sorry."

Mercy screamed as Capt. Davis snapped her toe back in place. Even with her eyes closed, she saw a white light flash. "Ooouchh," she groaned.

"I'm sorry. It was dislocated. In my experience it's better if the patient doesn't see it coming. Good news, it's set now, but you'd best stay off of it today and rest."

"What happened?!" Adelaide asked, rushing over.

Mercy shook her head. "The doctor was just setting my toe . . . and my perspective," she groaned.

"She'll have to stay off of it for a bit," Capt. Davis said.

"Will she have to stay here?" Adelaide asked.

"I should think not," Capt. Davis said, scooping Mercy off the cot. "I believe I can manage her back to the wagon."

"Yes, sir," Adelaide said. "I'll keep an eye on things till you get back."

Mercy's foot throbbed with each jarring step, but the cool wind blowing across the bare skin felt heavenly.

"I meant what I said earlier; I am truly sorry for offending you," he said.

"I wasn't mad at you, I was just foolishly taking it out on you," Mercy muttered. "I was mad things weren't going the way I wanted them to. Mad the king won't just give up, that the French can't just end the war, and that the redcoats won't just let my papa come home. I was mad that your pessimism was right, and my optimism was wrong. Again."

"My *realism* was right," Capt. Davis corrected.

Mercy clenched her teeth, glaring at him.

"Not that your optimism was wrong, only premature," he corrected.

Mercy shook her head. "What kind of gentleman are you?"

"Flawed, I'm afraid. My flaw being that I am most often . . . correct."

Mercy snorted, and Capt. Davis grinned.

"I knew you were in there somewhere," he smiled.

"Oh Lord," Abigail groaned, looking to the sky as they approached.

"It's nothing serious, ma'am," Capt. Davis assured. "There was an accident and Mercy dislocated her toe. It looks a bit gruesome, but if she can stay off it for a bit, she'll be right as rain."

"What kind of accident?" Abigail asked, covering her mouth at the sight.

"The foolish kind," Mercy answered.

"Well, you'd best lay her in the wagon if you're able."

Capt. Davis hefted her into the wagon and laid her down.

"Thank you, sir," Mercy said.

"I'll be by later to check on you."

"Oh, there's no need for that," Abigail said. "I've done plenty of nursing in my day."

Mercy frowned.

"Yes, ma'am." Capt. Davis bowed. "Best make it two days, and then go easy."

"She will," Abigail replied.

Abigail turned to Mercy as Captain Davis walked away. "Goodness, Mercy, the men are away at war and you're committing foolish accidents? You're supposed to be on my side."

"I'm sorry, Mama. I heard about the French ships sailing for Boston and I just got so mad I kicked a water pail."

"Did you learn your lesson?"

"Is that something that all mama's ask?! Is it like, written down somewhere or something?"

Abigail put her hands on her hips, raising her eyebrows.

"Yes, ma'am. I learned my lesson. Make sure the pail is empty next time."

"Mercy . . ."

"And maybe I need to get a handle on my temper."

"Does it hurt?" Abigail asked.

"More than you can imagine," Mercy groaned.

Chapter 14

Two weeks after the storms, Henry and Benjamin were back in camp. The siege, as a test of allied coordination, was an abysmal failure. The Americans had been forced to retreat when the British General Pigot realized he had the advantage and attacked. Losses on both sides had been minimal, but the redcoats had proven that though they were cornered, they were far from finished.

Sullivan berated the French with such harsh terms that the hot-headed Marquis de Lafayette was enraged and challenged the general to a pistol duel to once again defend his countrymen's honor. Fortunately, cooler heads prevailed, and no duel was necessary. It was a rocky start to what had been a promising alliance.

"So, are we winning or losing?" David asked as they sat around their fire for dinner.

"Winning," Henry said. "We've held the redcoats to the New York area. Retreat or not, they didn't gain any ground, but our strategy will need to be revised."

"Why don't they just quit?" Abigail muttered.

"Pride?" Henry suggested. "It feels as though they themselves are not quite sure what actions to take next."

"Will the French return?" Abe asked.

"I believe so, though they did not make so good a showing this time. The storm was brutal, perhaps the French commander knew his ships would be no match for the British in that condition and his retreat was for the best."

"Capt. Davis said Washington's spies reported that the British navy are anchored in New York Harbor for repairs as well," Mercy said.

"That seems to substantiate French claims," Benjamin said. "Still, I'm a little salty. General Sullivan said the siege was only days from success. Capturing Newport would have allowed us to further hamper British resupply, and that's the key to ending the war."

"My goodness, Ben," Adelaide fawned. "You sound like a general already."

Abigail smiled, squeezing Henry's arm, while Ben melted. It was pathetic . . . and adorable, how a mighty warrior could be felled by a single word from the one who held his heart. Mercy remembered how her mama used to do the same thing to her papa when he'd come in from a long day in the field. He was a strong, quiet man, but her praise could melt him like butter. It must be something God put in, that a man with all his strength, wisdom, and fury, could be soothed by the gentle words of the one he loved. Maybe, like the battered war ships, the Lord knew courageous men would need a harbor.

It was good to have them home again, with the firelight dancing on their faces, and Henry's pipe smoke enhancing the atmosphere. These were her favorite diary entries, the one's she would read again and again while they were away, reliving the moments until they returned.

It was also in these moments that she began to feel a strange loneliness. It seemed odd, with everyone present, but still, it was there. She shook the foolishness of it from her head, she'd pray about it later, surely God would know why it was there. Maybe it was just her heart missing her papa.

The following morning, she made her way to the medical tent alone. Adelaide and Ben had stayed up late talking by the fire, and

Abigail would want to have breakfast with Henry. It was early September and already there were signs that the seasons were changing. The baby geese that swam in the pond looked more like small versions of their parents now, than the little balls of fluff they'd been in the spring. Fawns frolicking beside their mothers were losing their spots. The mornings also began with a chill that was quickly driven away by the rising sun.

"Good morning, Mercy," Capt. Davis said, sipping his coffee. "It must be a relief to have your family back again."

"Yes, sir. Believe it or not, Abigail is sending the boys to catch more frogs today; she wants Henry and Benjamin to try them."

"I can. It is something one must experience in order to believe." He smiled.

"How are the patients this morning?"

"Most of them are doing well, though there are a couple of infections amongst those wounded in the retreat from Rhode Island."

"They're bad, aren't they?" Mercy asked. "You always look away when you're telling me bad news."

"Do I?" he scoffed, looking at his boots. "The one will need an amputation, and the other probably won't last the week."

"I'm sorry, sir."

"I dread the feel of it. . . . Sawing on a man's flesh, knowing at best he'll be maimed for life, and at worst he'll die on my table.

Save yourself from ever knowing it; like the frogs, it is a thing you will never forget."

Mercy's heart ached, and she regretted spoiling his peaceful morning by asking their condition. He had no one to praise his work after a long day, to heal him when he was battered, no harbor, no one.

"I'll help you," Mercy said. "I know Abigail usually does, but her stomach isn't what it used to be."

"You'll regret it."

"I'll regret it more if I don't."

Capt. Davis nodded, finishing his coffee. "Let's get to work then."

When it was over, Mercy sat by herself for a while. Capt. Davis was right; it was not a thing she would likely forget. Fortunately, the patient had passed out from shock part way through, but it was awful. If the man woke, he'd find a heavily bandaged nub where his foot had once been and weeks of painful healing if another infection didn't set in. It was a grim thing.

"He's resting peacefully now," Capt. Davis said, finding her near the fire. "Are you alright?"

"I don't know, but I've felt that way long before now. If to be alright means that it doesn't bother me, that I don't feel it, then I'd rather not be alright. I don't want to live a numb life; I want to live a full life. A life that feels . . . sometimes the bad things just feel really deep."

"I know what you mean. Would you care to take a walk?"

Mercy nodded, and he held out his hand, lifting her from the stump.

They set out along the edge of the training ground, passed beside the rows of white tents, stopped for a while to admire the cavalry horses. The sun warmed their battered souls, the rich smells of woodsmoke comforted them in its embrace, and the courageous steeds who'd born their riders into countless battles looked on them with understanding.

"Horses are wise," Mercy said. "You can see it in their eyes, it's almost as if they were speaking to me."

"Aye, they are. I always talk to the horses when my heart is heavy."

"Does it help?"

"Well . . ." Capt. Davis straightened. "They're excellent listeners, and . . . most of the time I guess that is all I need. Probably seems foolish."

"No . . . It's the same for me when I write to my papa in my diary. I know he can't answer back, but still it helps."

"The heart is a complex thing. It can endure all that we have endured, but it has its limits."

"The horses seem quite fixated with you," Mercy said.

"I've spent a fair amount of time talking with them over the past few years . . ." Captain Davis said, reaching up and petting one on the neck. "Though today I forgot to bring any apples," he chuffed.

Mercy smiled. "I'll bet my brothers are down at the stream catching frogs, it's hilarious to watch."

"Sounds like a welcome distraction," Capt. Davis agreed.

Making their way down to the stream, they were met with the shrieks and shouts of the younger Bells and Youngs splashing about the shoreline grasses. Mable screamed helplessly as she tried to contain a water pail full of frogs that had no intention of staying for dinner. Nathaniel, Abe, and David were dripping from head to toe in hot pursuit of another large amphibian as Mercy and Capt. Davis made the stream.

"Ah, this is much more entertaining than staying in camp," Capt. Davis beamed, taking in the pandemonium.

Presently, the boys' quarry turned back upstream, hopping straight for them through the marsh grasses. Mercy jumped back to avoid being splashed, but Capt. Davis lunged for the creature. As his hands grasped around the frog, he lost his footing, plunging headlong into the stream.

Mercy gasped, and the boys froze their pursuit.

After a couple of moments, he sputtered to the surface still clutching the frog, and burst out laughing. Wiping his face with his sleeve, he handed the frog to Abe. "Well, it looks like I'm committed now, would you mind hanging up my stockings and shoes to dry?"

"I don't mind at all," Mercy smiled, holding out her hand to help pull him from the water.

Capt. Davis pulled off his shoes and stockings, and Mercy hung them on a nearby shrub. Then, he darted back into the water after the boys. Mercy wandered over to Mable and picked some reeds to weave into a cover for the pail. She'd never seen this side of him before, laughing and playing; for once he actually seemed . . . young.

When the pail could hold no more frogs, the boys took to wrestling one another, which evolved into the boys vs. Capt. Davis. Mable cheered on the boys while Mercy cheered on the captain. At times Capt. Davis was teetering in the water with a boy on both legs and one on his back, but all the while he was laughing and antagonizing the boys with playful banter.

"They'll all smell better after today," Mable smiled.

"That's the truth," Mercy agreed.

When at last the battling was done, the men came shore to allow the sun to dry their linen shirts and breeches as best it could before starting back to camp with their bounty. The boys and

Mable ran ahead with the frogs while Mercy and Capt. Davis brought up the rear.

"I didn't know you knew how to do anything besides work," Mercy jested.

"There's a first time for everything," Capt. Davis replied.

"You're kidding!"

Capt. Davis sighed. "Only son from a wealthy family . . . it was all duty and discipline for me, I'm afraid."

"You never played?"

"Oh, I'm sure I did some as a small child, though I don't remember it."

"I can't imagine not having gone on so many adventures and the like with my siblings. Life would seem so tedious and boring."

"Much like myself?" he asked, lifting an eyebrow.

"Well, no . . . I mean, sometimes maybe," Mercy winced.

Capt. Davis chuffed. "That's one of the things I've always appreciated about you, your honesty."

"But you were different today," she smiled. "You seemed happy."

"I am. It was a grand adventure, in fact, it was just the medicine I needed. I can see why you have so much hope for life after the war, for me, the war is a distraction from my life."

"You don't have to live that way. . . . After we've won you can live however you'd like."

"I don't know what my life will be like if we win. My father has too much pride, we may never see each other again. And as for the rest of my family, I've failed everyone's expectations. I'm afraid following my conscience has made me a bit of an outcast."

"You're not an outcast to us. Maybe you also need to let go of your old world in order to have a new one. Just like we're shrugging off the redcoats and putting on something new. I'm sure we could find room for a good doctor in Cambridge."

"I hear you were of service for our dinner tonight," Abigail said when they reached the wagon.

"The boys did most of the work," Capt. Davis bowed.

"Well, all the same, you should join us," Abigail said.

"I appreciate the offer, ma'am, but I'm afraid I must see to my patient. The first few days are the worst," he said, bowing again.

"We'll be praying," Abigail replied.

"Thank you," Capt. Davis replied, before setting off for the medical tent.

"I heard Jonathan Bell's unit is back, perhaps we should invite the Bells," Henry suggested.

"I'll send Benjamin to fetch them," Abigail said.

Chapter 15

With the redcoats trapped in New York, life was able to return to a level of normal none of them had known since Cambridge. Their days fell into a routine, and while the two armies continued to probe one another in the no-man's-land between them, life in camp was peaceful.

It was just this kind of normal that stirred Mercy's heart for the kinds of adventures they'd had before, and so, on this beautiful mid-September day, after she'd finished her duties, she dusted off her snares and set out to find some fellow adventurers.

She collected Adelaide from the cauldron, then Abe and David, who invited Nathaniel and Mable, and then Benjamin who suggested they invite Jonathan. They departed the camp heading along the stream, looking for the tell-tale signs of rabbits.

"Seems a might strange for young ladies to be setting snares," Jonathan commented.

"We've had to learn to do a lot of things since all our men have been off to war," Adelaide said.

"We're still here," Abe balked.

"Well, most of the men," Adelaide corrected.

"I suppose it hasn't been easy, especially with Pa gone," he replied.

"Mercy says that Indian girls know how to trap and fish," Mable said.

"That's what Mr. Hadley tells me," Mercy said.

"Of course they do, they're savages," Jonathan replied.

"Well, then I guess I'm a savage too," Mercy quipped.

"That's not what I meant," Jonathan replied. "Mama says your wild ways have helped keep you all fed better than most in our absence. I just hope you can remember what it is to be a woman when this is all over."

"Perhaps they're one and the same for the native girls," Mercy answered.

"This looks like a good spot," Ben cut in.

They'd arrived at a thick blackberry patch with a few distinct tunnels leading in and out of it. Mercy uncoiled her snares, and she, Adelaide, and Ben set to work setting them.

"If you'd walk me through it, I'd be willing to set it for you," Jonathan said.

"That's alright," Mercy replied, "I enjoy it."

"I'd like to know how it is done, all the same," he said, kneeling next to her. "I was never taught."

"It's quite simple really. We look for thick areas like this, or a blowdown from the storm. You can see these little tunnels where the rabbits sneak in and out of the patch. It takes a little practice, but soon you start to see them everywhere."

She continued to explain the process, answering his questions as best she could. When it came to bending the sapling, Jonathan doubled one over for her with ease. Then she set the trigger and tested it with a stick so he could understand how it all worked.

"It's simple, yet brilliant," Jonathan said, after they'd reset the snare and Mercy had disguised the noose with dried grass.

"We'll set several before heading back; that way we'll have better odds of catching one or two."

"Ours is all set," Ben said, dusting off his breeches.

"I'd like to try and set one if I could," Jonathan said.

"Let's find another patch," Mercy suggested.

A ways further down the trail, they found a large blowdown where several trees had fallen together. Mercy uncoiled her snares again and handed one to Jonathan. She watched him study the tangle of sticks and leaves. He was slightly bigger than Ben, not much taller, but with a bigger frame. His hands were thick and strong as he rolled the wire in his fingers. He had a rounder face, his features not so well defined as Ben's, but he looked like he could carry a cannon.

His unit had always been deployed elsewhere and she'd never gotten to know him like the rest of the Bells. She had not so much as uttered a word to him before pulling him from that storm a year ago. Now the weight of the Bell family was on his shoulders.

"Is this a good spot?" he asked nervously, pointing to a circular opening in the tangle.

"That's where I'd put it," Mercy smiled.

He nodded, kneeling down to set the snare. Mercy watched him work the wire as she had done. He found a suitable trigger stick, bent the sapling, set the snare, shaped the loop and disguised it with dry pine needles.

"That looks perfect," Ben said.

Jonathan nodded, standing up to admire his work.

"I expect we'll find a hare in that soon," Mercy agreed.

On the way back, Mercy followed the pack of adventurers; the younger ones always competing to get back to camp first, Ben and Adelaide walking shoulder to shoulder unaware there was anyone else in the world, and Mercy lost in her own ponderings taking in the beauty of the world around her. It wasn't until he cleared his throat that she even realized he was there. Glancing up, she noticed Jonathan's eyes dart away from her nervously.

"I never got the chance to thank you for saving me that day in the storm," he said.

"Yes, you did, before they sent you home to recover," Mercy said.

"I must not have had my wits about me; I have no memory of it. I didn't want you to think me ungrateful."

"You're Adelaide's brother, I couldn't have left you there," Mercy said.

"But you had orders."

"And I followed them. You've made a full recovery and have returned to the line."

"You didn't know that when you saved me."

"No . . . I didn't. Your family is a part of my family . . . I couldn't have left you out there. No order in the world could convince me to do that. I thought Capt. Davis would have a fit, but he understood."

"He's a good doctor."

"He is." Mercy smiled. "He'd love to hear that from you. It's grim work he does, and there's not much praise for it."

"I'll try and get over there to tell him."

They continued along the stream to the marshy area where the boys and Capt. Davis had caught their frogs. The younger ones had already made it back to camp where they were sure to be bored and regret their haste before the others even showed up. Mercy jumped as a large bullfrog leapt from the grasses just ahead of her and splashed into the stream. She held her hand to her chest as she caught her breath.

"Who knew those things could be so tasty?" Jonathan said.

"I wish we would have eaten that one." Mercy smiled ruefully.

"Would you like me to catch him for you?"

"No . . . I tend to be a bit vengeful," Mercy said. "At least that's what Henry tells me. But I'm working on it."

"Mama says you've got plenty of vinegar, and she'd know, she's got plenty herself. My Pa would say it was one of the things he missed the least and the most about Mama when we were away."

"I'm sorry he's gone."

"Me too. We worked together for so long . . . it was always the two of us, figuring everything out. Now I'm just left with Mama."

"Just? Your mama is one of the most independently stubborn women I've ever met, but she lives up to her responsibilities better than I ever could. She's kept herself and your family together through all the struggles we've endured, most of the time while you were all away. Your struggles end at the battlefield while hers never end. Yet she rises every day to see to them, and the needs of others, with tireless resolve. You'd have to be a blind man to think you were carrying on alone and fail to appreciate all that Mrs. Bell carries."

Jonathan looked down at her wide-eyed. "Are you always this forward?"

"I thought you'd be used to it."

"Well, yes, that's because she's my mother, but she'd never be so forward with Pa."

"Would you rather I'd let you go on thinking incorrectly?"

Again, he looked at her perplexed. "I don't think it's your place—"

"Henry says a wise man appreciates the gift of truth however he finds it, while the fool can't get past the wrappings," Mercy said.

"And you think I'm a fool?"

"If you're too proud to accept the truth."

Jonathan snorted. "And Henry encourages you to always speak your mind?"

"When it's appropriate, though he has taught me that there are times when I need to bite my tongue, and let me tell you, there have been times my tongue has been plenty sore."

"I can imagine. With a wit as quick as yours it's unlikely a girl like you would even pause to consider her words before she spoke, without someone telling her to."

"And what's that supposed to mean?!" Mercy glared at him.

"Only that, like the many young women I've observed, you seem to think the only reason God gave you a tongue is for nagging and gossiping. And if that's the case, then wouldn't it be altogether wiser if you remained silent?"

Mercy felt her cheeks flush.

"Don't get caught up in the wrappings." He bowed and turned away, setting off into camp.

Mercy glared at his back as he went, grinding her teeth. So, this is the man she rescued.

"You two seemed to be getting along grand," Adelaide beamed. "That's the most I've seen him talk to anyone in years, especially a young lady."

Lifting her dress, Mercy turned and marched past Adelaide, back to their wagon. As she neared it, her eyes locked on a lone water pail. Marching up to it, she cocked her leg back, and with fists clenched she prepared to send it into kingdom come.

"Oh, no you don't, Mercy Young!" Abigail called from the wagon.

Mercy froze, glaring at her target.

Abigail climbed out from the wagon, rushing over to her. "What's gotten into you, love? Have you already forgotten what happened the last time? You're still walking with a bit of a limp for goodness sake!"

Mercy dropped her foot, still seething.

"Now tell me. What's all this about?"

Mercy shook her head.

"Come on . . . out with it," Abigail said, guiding Mercy down onto one of the stumps by the fire.

"Fine! That daft Jonathan Bell told me that all I do is gossip and nag and it'd be better if I was silent," Mercy muttered.

"Didn't you save his life last season?"

"Yes! Ungrateful wretch, should've just left him there. . ."

"Mercy Young!" Abigail gasped. "Take that back at once, there's no offence he could have delivered deserving of death, child."

"He compared me to the likes of those foolish girls who swoon over General Lafayette!"

"Mercy."

"Fine! I take it back . . . but I no longer accept his belated appreciation of my efforts. Mock my quick wit—well it was that quick wit that pulled you out of that storm!" Mercy shouted. "Oohh, it just makes me want to call fire down on him . . . He said I don't think before I speak!" Mercy said, throwing up her hands.

Abigail looked at her in amazement.

"What?!" Mercy asked.

"I don't think you should work so hard to prove him correct, Mercy."

"Argh! You didn't hear him, Mama!"

"Mercy, you have to remember, not everyone is brought up the way you were. The Puritans are a different breed altogether, from their clothes to their rules. In their culture, a woman's place is to be quiet, submissive, plain, and proper at all times. Not *all* bad qualities, perhaps a bit overly rigid, but that is the only world he knows. You must understand that for a young lady to voice her opinion without being expressly asked for it is a new notion for him, and one he probably finds distasteful."

"Well, I find him distasteful," Mercy muttered.

"Who'd have guessed. . . ."

"So, I'm the one in the wrong?" Mercy groaned.

"I didn't say that, Mercy. I just think you've had a misunderstanding because the two of you see the world differently, just like when we first met Mrs. Bell."

"Who knew there could be anyone worse?"

"Mercy . . ."

"I like her now, I just meant at first."

"And if you'd called fire down on her, where would our friendship be? Your temper is like a tempest, Mercy. You've got to learn to ride out the storm without kicking buckets or charring folks, or in the end you'll be the one who gets hurt."

"How come Capt. Davis's flaw is that he's always right, and mine is that I'm always wrong," Mercy pouted.

"I didn't say *you* were wrong, only your response to the offense. You give folks entirely too much say in your mind. You know who you are, Mercy Young, so why does it matter so much if others do not?" Abigail said, lifting her chin.

Mercy relaxed her shoulders. "I don't know. . . ."

"Well, messing up your foot again certainly isn't going to help."

"I know," Mercy chuffed. "That little voice inside was screaming for dear life, but I wasn't listening."

Abigail pulled her in close.

"I just want to cry. . . ."

"I know," Abigail said, planting a kiss on top of her head. "These years are hard years for a young lady, and to have to live through them during a war . . . it isn't fair, it isn't fair at all."

Chapter 16

Mercy had already completed her rounds on the morning of September 28th when a great commotion in the camp drew her out of the tent. The sound of clomping hooves and clattering wagon wheels rapidly approaching spelled trouble.

"What's the devil done now?" Capt. Davis groaned as the wagon pulled to a stop.

Mercy and Capt. Davis raced to the wagon with Adelaide on their heels. On the flatbed lay more than a dozen Continentals, bayonetted and slashed.

"It was that General Grey again!" shouted the driver hopping down. "He found General Baylor's boys sleeping last night and had at 'em. They only left the dead and dying behind—took the rest! Judging by the mess, a lot of them captured boys are hurt pretty bad. General Baylor and his staff are presumed captured as well."

Capt. Davis looked grimly at Mercy. "Let's get these boys inside. Adelaide, prepare some cots and bring the whiskey."

Gingerly they carried the five remaining survivors inside; the rest would go to the grave diggers. Three of the men had already lost consciousness, the other two teetered on the edge. Even as they were placed on the cots, she knew their conditions were hopeless.

"Hello, sir," Mercy said, leaning over one of the conscious patients, while Capt. Davis looked over the other.

The boy didn't answer. He was around Ben's age, twenty at most. A newer recruit based on the condition of his shoes and uniform, perhaps this had even been his first contact with the enemy. A boy, probably as zealous as her brothers, not wanting to miss his chance at fighting in freedom's war.

She took his hand and held it as a single tear rolled down his cheek. "You're not alone . . ." she whispered, her own eyes filling with tears.

"This one's gone," she heard Capt. Davis say, and one of the other patients was carried out the flap. A few moments later, the next was carried out.

She prayed desperately, clinging to the boy's hand. His linen shirt was soaked with maroon blood from where a bayonet had pierced his lower abdomen. She knew there was nothing she could do, nothing could change what was coming, all because they'd gone to sleep near where that barbarous General Grey was prowling.

"He's gone, Mercy," Capt. Davis said.

She stopped praying, looking down into his lifeless brown eyes. It was over. Before she could even fight, his battle had already been decided. Laying his hand down beside him, she closed his eyes, releasing one final tear to roll down his cheek.

"I'm sorry," he said.

"I know . . . I'm sorry too."

"None of them had a chance. That General Grey is a monster, I pray they boil him in oil should we ever capture him," Capt. Davis said. "First the Paoli Massacre, and now this—he's not a man!"

Looking across the room, she saw Adelaide sitting beside the cot of a man whose chest still rose and fell, but his head had clearly suffered a significant fracture from the butt of a musket. With injuries of this kind, it was unlikely he would ever wake, and the ones who did were rarely ever right again.

Losses like these made up the bulk of her nightmares. She could understand the losses on the battlefield, and in a way, make sense of them. But to see boys murdered in their sleep, without honor or decorum; her mind couldn't accept it. And to know that General Grey was still lurking out there somewhere . . . how could anyone sleep peacefully?

Word of General Grey's second massacre sent shockwaves through the camp. The majority of soldiers and officers alike demanded retaliation. It would seem a dishonor to General Baylor and his men if the redcoats were able to commit such atrocities without retribution.

The massacre cast a cloud over the rest of the day, and by the end only the patient with the head injury remained. There was no word yet on the rest of Baylor's men, or even Baylor himself, and Washington had yet to give orders. The year that had started so promising was turning into a frustrating disappointment.

On Mercy's way back to the wagon, she met Henry returning from drill.

"I heard it was a bitter day for you all," he said.

"A bitter day for all of us," Mercy replied. "How could a man do such a dishonorable thing to another?"

"I can't imagine it," Henry agreed. "I did hear that General Washington believes General Clinton aimed to provoke us into battle. Our alliance with the French is on shaky ground, their fleet is still in Boston for repairs, and his position is strong. Spies claim he is confident in his army and believes he'd win such an engagement."

"Well, the camp seems to be pretty provoked, that's for sure. Do you think they would win?"

"I think they have the advantage if it were to be fought on their ground, but they must feel the same about fighting on our ground because they haven't come out to meet us here either."

"It seemed so simple if the French fleet hadn't been damaged," Mercy sighed. "Why didn't God just give us that victory?"

"I don't know . . ." Henry said, wrapping an arm around her.

"I've cried so many tears these past few years. . . ."

"I'm sure the Good Lord has counted each one of them precious and will reward you for them one day."

Mercy leaned into him, and he held her tightly. "Mama says that tears are prayers from our souls when words are unable to express how deeply we feel."

"Sounds right," Henry smiled.

When they reached the wagon, Mercy was delighted to find that the boys had checked the snares, and they would be having rabbit stew for dinner. For some reason a belly full of warm food had a comforting effect on the soul. Then she found out the Bells would be joining them for dinner—all of the Bells.

The Bells were served first, as they were guests, and took their seats on the stumps and barrels around the fire. Mercy had volunteered to serve everyone, leaving her the last to dish up, a tactical error she observed, as there was only one seat left, the stump beside Jonathan Bell.

In a moment of panic, she glanced around the circle looking for another option, anything would be better than sitting beside her nemesis; she'd sit on a cactus if it meant not sitting beside him.

"What on earth are you waiting for, Mercy?" Abigail chided.

"Oh, I was thinking I'd sit in the buckboard and eat with Theo," she said. "It's been a hard day and I find him very comforting."

"Nonsense," Abigail said. "You've eaten with him on your shoulder plenty of times, there's no reason you can't eat and fellowship with the rest of us. Now, sit down so Henry can give the blessing."

Mercy did as she was told. Trudging over to the stump, she called to Theo, and sat down in a humph. Henry gave the blessing, praying for the families of those who'd perished, and asking the Lord not to desert those who'd been captured. Mercy found herself distracted with fantasies of Theo pouncing on Jonathan and flying off with an ear.

"Amen," Henry said, and Mercy shook herself from her thoughts.

She stared intently at her bowl as she took the first bite, feeling Theo track it lustfully from the bowl to her mouth. She pled in her mind with each bite that Jonathan wouldn't speak to her, that they'd just eat their food and go their separate—

"It's horrible, what happened today," Jonathan said.

Mercy went stiff but pretended not to hear him. She took another bite.

"I remember being in the medical tent, it couldn't have been easy for you," he continued.

She took another bite, willing Theo to pounce on him.

"I hope we can capture that dreadful General Grey. What do you think would be a just punishment for such a creature?" he asked.

Mercy cringed. *Not a question!* He was trying to force her to participate!

There was an awkward silence as Mercy took another bite, and then another. Thanks to her current company, she was hardly able to enjoy the sweet, warm, savor of the stew.

"Are you refusing to converse with me?" he asked.

Yes! Mercy clenched her jaw, before taking another bite.

"Seems very childish for a young lady who's about to be sixteen, but I suppose one must expect any manner of foolishness from a *girl* who still talks to animals."

Fire. Red hot fire rose from her belly and surged through every fiber of her being. She turned to face him for the first time, her face contorting into a grimace as she held her spoon like a dagger, pointing it at his chest.

"I'm sorry, your highness, but I got the impression you preferred me SILENT!" she snapped, louder than she'd intended.

Everyone broke off their conversations, staring at them.

"And I'd rather talk to an owl to the end of my days, than the arrogant likes of you!" Mercy seethed.

It was too late to turn back now; standing from her stump, Mercy turned and stormed away into the darkness.

Abigail called after her, but she heard Henry tell her to let her go. She wouldn't cry, not this time, she wouldn't give him the satisfaction. How could anyone be so infuriating? She stopped for a moment to thank God again for not letting the Bells find them. She couldn't imagine living in their world. How had Adelaide survived?

She wandered away from the tents, the fires, and the din of the camp. She needed to breathe, needed clean crisp air, and the comforting freedom of being alone. She made her way down the valley by the light of the moon, ignoring the dew that dampened her hem. Billions of stars filled a never-ending sky overhead in breathtaking fashion, while a host of amphibians and insects sang like a choir from the marshy shore of the stream.

Finding the log the boys had acquired for Adelaide and herself, she sat down. It was then that she noticed she'd carried her bowl of stew the entire way, and it had unfortunately grown cold.

"Here," she said, setting the bowl beside her on the log. "You can have the rest."

Theo hopped off her shoulder and circled the bowl a couple times before sticking his beak inside and pulling out a scrap of rabbit.

"He's not wrong, Theo. I would very much rather talk to you than him. You don't think that makes me odd, do you?"

Theo looked up at her for a moment as if to say, "No." And then returned to his scavenging in the bowl.

"I think it's odd to be altogether insulting and then still expect a perfectly rational girl to want to converse with you. If I were a boy, I could just bop him on the nose and no one would think anything of it, but if a lady so much as refuses to speak to a man, even if she has good reason, then she's the one who's being improper."

She kicked a pebble into the water and watched the ripples dance in the moonlight. They were probably all sitting around the fire discussing her poor manners. Mrs. Bell shaking her head, while Abigail made excuses for her, Jonathan smiling smugly all the while. She'd surely get an earful from Abigail when she returned.

"Oh, Mercy," she'd say. "If you didn't want to talk to the boy, you should have just told him, there was no cause for making a scene. You really must learn to control your temper."

She'd be right of course, except that telling him she didn't want to talk to him was more talking than Mercy felt he deserved.

Thus, he got silence . . . just what he'd asked for. And yet, when she returned, she'd be the one saying sorry.

"It isn't fair, Theo. I wish we could just trade places. You be the girl for a while, and I'll be an owl."

Theo didn't look up from his rummaging through the contents of her bowl.

"I knew you'd say that . . . you've got it too easy. You could defend me once in a while, you know. You wouldn't have had to take the whole ear, just a piece of it."

She stayed until the guilt of knowing Abigail was worrying about her drove her back to the wagon. By the time she arrived, everyone had already gone to bed except for Henry and Abigail. To her surprise, Abigail rose from her seat and rushed to look her over.

Satisfied, she took Mercy by the hands with an understanding smile and said, "Run along to bed, we can talk about it in the morning."

Something in the way she said it told Mercy that everything was going to be okay. Even if she had made a mistake, Abigail would always love her anyway. Setting Theo on the buckboard, she climbed inside the flap of the wagon.

Chapter 17

The following morning Mercy awoke early, slipped out of the
wagon, collected Theo, and prepared to set off for the creek
and the woods beyond to check her snares. She wanted to be
alone, to process the best way to make today less . . . awkward.

She placed a few dried pieces of kindling and a piece of
firewood on the smoldering coals to make Abigail's job easier
when she woke and turned to leave.

"Hey!" came a sharp whisper.

So much for being alone. Mercy turned and smiled at her
friend.

"I thought I saw you climbing from the wagon," Adelaide
smiled. "Where are you headed so early?"

"Oh, I was just about to check my snares before breakfast,"
Mercy said. "Just needed to take a walk."

"Mind if I join you?"

"No, I don't mind," Mercy lied.

They remained quiet until they'd reached the edge of camp and started down the hill towards the stream. Mercy could feel the uncomfortable conversation brewing between them, she'd created tension between their families and now they'd have to work it out.

"I'm sorry my brother got under your skin last night," Adelaide said at last.

Mercy cringed. *Here it comes.* . . .

"He's not real adept at relationships. I think papa was the only person he ever felt he could be himself around. Before the war, all any of us knew was our community of rules, propriety, and perfection. We knew our place there; to us, the way we lived was *normal*. Puritans are not bad people, Mercy, just because we're different. But I think we followed the letter of our rules blindly for so long we forgot the heart behind them."

"And what's that?" Mercy asked.

"To honor the Lord and our fellow man. But we're humans, and I can see how we've allowed our rules to make us little better than the pharisees. That's why I've made it my aim to follow His word from my heart, rather than my head. Jonathan—he's a young man, and he wants to be approved of, like we all do. In our world, that's done by piously following our rules. The way we dress, the way we act, the way we obey. In our world women are quiet, respectful, and submissive when dealing with men . . . even when wronged. He's never met a girl who speaks her mind like you do. And in our world, if a man can't keep a lady in her place, he's a poor excuse of a man."

"I'm not his lady!" Mercy snapped.

"No, but I think . . . I think maybe he'd like you to be."

"What?!"

"I was trying to tell you that after we'd set the snares! I've never, and I mean never, seen him talk to a young lady in my life! He hardly talks to men! I think he's fond of you."

"He doesn't even know me!"

"No, but I think he's beginning to. Since papa died, and he's the man of the family now . . . I think he's looking for someone to help him."

Mercy caught herself against a tree to keep from falling over. "This is madness," she gasped.

"He even defended you to Mama last night. He said it was all his fault and that you were right to storm off," Adelaide said.

Mercy's head spun; this couldn't be happening. In all her imaginations of how this situation would play out, this scenario had never even entered her mind, and she had an extraordinary imagination. He couldn't have affections for her; they hadn't had more than five conversations and over half of them had ended poorly.

"Are you alright?" Adelaide asked.

"No . . ." Mercy groaned. "Can't you convince him this is a terrible idea?"

"I think you've been doing a pretty good job of that yourself," Adelaide said.

"Right?! You can see this is all wrong, the circumstances, timing . . . the people! Can't you?"

"For goodness sakes, Mercy, he's not asking to marry you! He just wants a chance to get to know you. He's . . . interested, that's all."

Mercy nodded. "You're right, I've got plenty of time to dispel him of this notion."

Adelaide chuffed, "Or he'll dispel you of yours."

Mercy clung to the tree again, causing Theo to flap his wings irritably trying to find proper footing.

"I'm sorry, Adelaide. I'm happy for you and Ben, and I'm sure Jonathan is a fine person in some way, but I just can't see myself . . . a Bell."

"Don't fret yourself, Mercy. These things have a way of working themselves out one way or another."

"Who told you that?"

"My mama, when I told her about my feelings for Ben."

"Would you still like me if it didn't work out?" Mercy asked.

"Of course I would! I want you to be where you belong, Mercy. What kind of friend would I be if I didn't? I think you are both wonderful people, but I'm not about to start pretending I know better than Jehovah."

Mercy breathed a sigh of relief, releasing the tree.

"All I ask is that you treat him fairly," Adelaide said, taking Mercy's hands.

Mercy nodded resolutely. "Okay . . ." She swallowed hard. "I will."

"Alright," Adelaide smiled. "Let's check the snares and get back before Mama starts worrying about me."

When they returned a while later with a plump rabbit, Abigail was already up working the fire Mercy had stoked. Adelaide bid her farewell, and Mercy turned to face her second awkward conversation of the day.

"Sorry I didn't tell you before I went off," Mercy said. "I just needed to think."

"It's alright," Abigail said. "I've known you long enough now to know that if you were to be attacked by a bear, I should be more worried for the bear."

"Was I that bad last night?" Mercy winced.

"Well, you left everyone speechless for a bit, but I have a feeling it may have been warranted."

"He's insufferable," Mercy said.

"I remember when you used to say that about his mother, but you've learned to see her differently now haven't you?"

"Adelaide thinks he's fond of me . . ."

"Ah, well, that does complicate things, doesn't it?" Abigail frowned.

Mercy nodded.

"But it doesn't really mean anything yet," Abigail said. "When I was younger, perhaps around your age, there was a handsome boy three years older than me who lived on one of the largest farms just outside of Boston. We'd find ways to spend time together every Sunday after church, just getting to know one another, of course. I even got caught sneaking out to meet him once."

"You?! Never!" Mercy gasped.

"Mm-hmm. I did. My father gave me a stern earful, and then marched over to his parent's farm to give him an earful. We weren't allowed to see each other for a number of weeks after that, except in passing at the church service."

"Was he . . . Mr. Henry?"

"No, dear, he wasn't. I thought we'd be a smart match, and he'd even gotten my father's permission to court me . . . after his temper had died down. It was bliss at first, and I was the envy of every eligible young lady in Boston, but as time went on, I found that I had to force myself to ignore the many ways in which we didn't fit. He had everything I'd thought I wanted, good looking, charming, came from a family more well to do than mine, but his character . . . it wasn't who he appeared to be on the outside."

"So, what happened?"

"I told my mother about his improprieties, and how they made me feel. She went to my father, and the courtship was broken off. We were the talk of the town for a short while, and many an airy older woman turned up their noses at me for passing up an opportunity to marry well."

"That must have been humiliating," Mercy groaned.

"It was . . . and yet, I've never once regretted it," Abigail smiled.

"How could you? You got Mr. Henry," Mercy agreed.

"It wasn't easy, though. Henry, while quietly charming, and handsome, was poor—nearly broke when we began courting. We were older, folks were starting to say I'd turn out an old maid, I was nearly twenty-eight. Henry had worked in the Boston shipyards, he was good at fixing things, building things, moving freight, and in the evenings, he'd serve at the tavern there. He didn't get paid much, but he saved every bit he could, not spending hardly a thing on food or lodging, he slept in a hammock in the yards."

"No wonder a soldier's life doesn't seem to be a hardship to him," Mercy said.

"Then one day, he surprised everyone, he took all that money he'd been saving and built the tavern. I can still see the look on my father's face when he came and asked his blessing to marry me. My father apologized for misjudging him and gave his blessing on the spot. We were married a month later and have worked side by side to turn the tavern into our dream for nearly ten years."

"That's amazing," Mercy said.

"And so will your story be, Mercy. Don't rush it, and don't run from it, just . . . let it be," Abigail said. "And as far as Jonathan Bell goes, don't worry, I don't think Henry will be giving you up to anyone without a fight."

Mercy snorted. "Thanks, Mama."

"Now, get cleaned up and help me with breakfast."

Mercy hung the rabbit on the wagon for one of her brothers to process and washed her hands in the basin. So far, the two conversations she'd had, while shocking, had not been negative. She was *trying* to just "let it be," but people were getting in the way of that. Why did growing up have to be so complicated? In a couple of weeks, she'd be sixteen, and one thing she knew for sure, she was *not* Mary Hays.

Chapter 18

October 15, 1778

I feel as though we are living in one of my nightmares. Only just this morning, another massacre took place not far from here at a place called Little Egg Harbor. It was a small outpost, only fifty men. A Tory militia set in on them while they slept. Reports say over forty-five perished of their bayonet wounds, the rest are presumed captured.

While it was not the vile General Grey this time, we can only assume it was his tactics. This level of dishonorable brutality has set off retaliatory skirmishes: neighbors, Tory and Patriot, burning, looting, and killing in the name of revenge. Redcoats or not, it seems we are aptly capable of destroying ourselves.

If General Clinton is indeed using these atrocities to provoke us to battle, he is a far less noble a man than his predecessor.

Washington, on the other hand, is resolute as ever to contain the redcoats until the French can cut off their supply be sea. His inaction has many a man and woman sorely questioning his leadership. I, for one, fully appreciate his unwillingness to risk lives without having every advantage.

Tomorrow is my birthday, and my only wish will be that the war comes to an end soon. This year I am blessed to spend my birthday with all of my loved ones close at hand, except for Papa. I am truly grateful that so many of us have survived thus far; countless folks have suffered many more losses than we have.

I face the morning with a sense of trepidation, the boys have been most mysterious lately, and I have no illusions they do not intend to surprise me in some way, be it good or evil. The two of them are infinitely creative, and menacingly devious when they are of the mind to be. I wouldn't put it past them to gift me a box of snakes.

When Benjamin turned eighteen in September, the boys gave him a half-used bar of soap and told him, in front of everyone, that he should use it as soon as possible so Adelaide didn't have to work so hard to find a place to sit upwind of him. He'd turned red as a beet but remained gracious and appreciative, more so than I would have been. I do believe he took their advice; he did seem fresher the following morning.

Come what may, I rejoice in another year that we are all still here. I look to the following year with hope, knowing many changes and challenges await me, but I am never alone. The Good Lord has brought me this far, surely, He will lead me a year more.

Mercy Young, 15 years old.

Contrary to her fears, the morning began without a hitch; the sun was shining, birds were singing, and breakfast was fried ham and toasted bread with butter. Abigail had wished her a happy birthday, Benjamin and Henry had gone to drill, and the boys went about their chores. It was perfect . . . too perfect. She made her way over to the medical tent half expecting the sky to fall; it was never this perfect.

As she made the medical tent, Theo swooped in and took his position on the nearest flatbed where he could watch for rodents amongst the supplies and receive handouts from the girls and others who'd taken a liking to him.

Mercy reached up and stroked his head, "You haven't seen anything suspicious going on, have you?"

He closed his eyes, leaning into her gentle scratching.

"It's my birthday, Theo, and I know those boys are up to something. I need you to be on the lookout for me, alright?"

He turned his cheek to her so she could scratch that, and she did.

"Good morning, Mercy," Adelaide said as she arrived. "Today is your birthday, isn't it?"

"It is," Mercy smiled.

Adelaide looked around to make sure no one was watching, then she took a small parcel from her shawl and slipped it to Mercy. "Happy birthday," she whispered.

Mercy peeled back the paper to reveal a novel titled The Expedition of Humphry Clinker, by a man named Mr. Smollett.

"Have you read it?" Adelaide asked excitedly.

"No, I've never seen it before, thank you!"

"I hear it's a hilarious story," she said.

"You've not read it?" Mercy asked.

"I'm not allowed to. . . ."

"Well, when we can find time to slip away, I'll read it to you . . . that way you haven't read it yourself," Mercy said, with a wink. "Where'd you get it?"

"I did some mending for one of Benjamin's officers and he traded the book to me for the work."

"Thank you," Mercy said, giving Adelaide a hug.

"Do you ladies intend to while away the entire morning with idle gossip?" Capt. Davis said from the flap.

"Do you always have to be such a grump?" Mercy asked. "It's my birthday."

Capt. Davis smiled. "I knew that would get a rise out of you."

Mercy rolled her eyes, ducking inside the flap. The tent was mostly empty, only a few patients likely to return to the field remained, the rest had been sent away to recover so they wouldn't bog down the army. Mercy reached the first patient only to find his bandages had already been changed, and he'd already had his needs tended to. So, she moved to the next, only to find the same, and on to the next.

Looking back at Capt. Davis, she caught him grinning slyly. "You've already seen to them all?" Mercy asked.

"Happy birthday, Mercy," he said.

"Thank you, sir. But what am I and Adelaide to do now?"

"I'm surprised the ever-adventurous Mercy Young would be want for ideas, but I'm glad you asked. I believe your brothers have prepared something for you down by the stream," he said.

"Oh, boy," Mercy said, raising an eyebrow and glancing at Adelaide.

The girls thanked Capt. Davis, hung up their aprons, and started for the stream. "I'm kind of glad we don't celebrate birthdays," Adelaide said. "This seems stressful."

"But worth it," Mercy said, putting on a brave face.

"Here she comes!" came Abe's whisper as they approached.

Mercy took one last brave look at Adelaide before rounding the bend.

"Surprise!" the boys shouted.

There, in their favorite spot, the boys had set up canes for fishing, moved her sitting long to the best spot, and started a small fire to break the morning chill. Abe and David smiled at her with excitement.

"Happy birthday, Mercy," David said.

"*Wow*," she said, taking it all in. "Thank you, boys."

"Why'd ya say it like that?" Abe asked, putting his hands on his hips. "What did you *think* we had planned?"

"Well," Mercy swallowed hard, "one year you did give me back my own diary after reading it. . . ."

"Mercy! That was ages ago," Abe complained.

"I know. I really appreciate this, boys. It's perfect."

Abe dropped his hands, smiling. "Told ya, Dave."

Mercy and Adelaide made their way to the log.

"Here, Mercy, you should take this one," David said, handing her one of the canes. "Oh . . . look, I think there's something on it already," he said, a little too obviously.

Mercy lifted the cane, and sure enough, there was a weight on it alright, but it didn't really fight back. She lifted the cane still further, drawing her line towards the shore. A few feet out she could see a large silvery fish gliding towards them along the surface. Abe looked at her with an uneasy smile.

When her line reached the shore, Abe lifted the fish for her. It was a large trout, but it had clearly passed away sometime earlier.

"What do ya think about that, Mercy!" David asked excitedly.

Mercy ruffled his hair. "It's a beaut', Dave. Thank you."

"I'll rebait your hook for you," Abe said, a little disappointed.

It was obvious the boys had caught the fish earlier in the morning and placed it on her line when they'd seen her coming. Somehow during the process, the poor creature had died, but the effort they'd put in on her behalf made it special all the same.

David's cane began to bounce, and he raced away to retrieve it.

"That fish must have put up a magnificent fight," Mercy whispered to Abe.

"It did." He smiled. "I nearly lost it in the weeds twice. I wanted to surprise you. . . ."

"You did a great job, Abe. I couldn't be happier, and to give me such a prize fish, dead or alive, means all the more. Much better than the diary," she smiled.

"Thanks," he said, giving her a rare hug.

"Let's catch a pile of fish for supper," she said. "I bet we can out-fish you . . . it's already one to nothing."

"What?!" Abe balked.

Mercy raised her eyebrows.

"Oh, yeah . . ." he blushed. "Okay, you're on!"

Mercy swung her line into the water, and Adelaide followed suit. The water was clear enough that, even with the ripples, the dark silhouettes of fish could be seen darting over the submerged leaf litter. It wasn't long and David's cane began to bounce again, and this time he was able to haul in a nice fish.

"That's one to one," Abe cheered.

It wasn't a minute before Abe's cane bent and he was in a fight with another good-sized fish.

"They're going to clobber us at this rate," Adelaide said.

"This is usually the best spot," Mercy groaned, then her tip began to bounce.

Mercy reached for her cane as Adelaide's nearly jumped from the fork. Both girls set the hooks and their battles began. Abe hauled his to shore and the boys took a short lead before the girls made the score three to two.

Theo glided in, having woken from his nap and immediately set in on Adelaide's fish, tangling himself in her line.

"Theo!" Mercy snapped, lunging for him.

He looked up at her with his big soulful eyes, pleading for rescue.

"Argh, you daft bird!" Mercy held him while Adelaide began untangling her line. "I thought you were supposed to be a wise owl, but you only think with your stomach!"

"Three to three!" Abe called out.

Adelaide worked frantically as Theo's head spun this way and that watching her curiously.

"Four to three!" hollered David.

"It's like a spiders web!" cried Adelaide, as she unwound one tangle only to find another.

"Watch his talons," Mercy coached.

"Five to three," Abe called.

"Theo! This is all your fault! Can't you just let me win on my birthday?!"

"I think I've almost got it!" Adelaide said. "Oh, wait . . . here's another tangle."

"Six to three!"

"Argh!" Mercy groaned.

"Okay, I've got it!" Adelaide said, letting her line drop free.

Mercy set Theo on the log. "Stay! And so help me—if you mess this up one more time, it's no fish for you!"

Theo looked up at her inquisitively.

"Seven to three!"

Mercy swung her line back out into the water and twitched it ever so slightly. It worked; a large trout nearly leapt from the water as it inhaled her hook. Rather than waste time fighting it, Mercy ran up the bank dragging the writhing fish to shore. Theo unfurled his wings but thought better of it when Mercy glared at him. She unhooked the fish and slipped it on the willow branch before tossing her line back into the water.

"I've got one too!" Adelaide said.

"Five to seven!" Mercy called.

"You mean five to eight," Abe said, landing his own fish.

The derby continued until the fish stopped biting around midday. Tragically, the girls were not able to overcome their deficit and lost by one. Even so, they were going home with a dozen large trout, and many laughs. Theo, though undeserving, was awarded a small fish because in the end, Mercy's feigned resentment had no spine.

When they arrived back at the wagon, Mercy was surprised to learn that Abigail and Mrs. Bell had gone to town, leaving Nathaniel and Mable to watch over things until the girls got back. Abigail rarely ever went to town, and she never went without Mercy. . . .

Chapter 19

At last evening came. Mercy had waited all afternoon on pins and needles waiting for everyone to return. Abigail had returned but wouldn't allow Mercy anywhere near the flatbed. Henry and Benjamin were also acting peculiar, and then she saw Mr. Hadley.

"What on earth are you doing here?" she asked, running to hug him.

He squeezed her tightly, looking down on her with his warm eyes. "I heard my sweet Mercy was becoming a lady. I wouldn't miss that birthday for the world."

Mercy smiled. "I'm the same girl I've always been."

"So, I've heard," he smiled back.

Abigail climbed out of the wagon, eyeing Mr. Hadley.

"Mrs. Tewksbury," Mr. Hadley said, tipping his hat.

"Mm-hmm," Abigail said.

Mr. Hadley looked at Mercy, confused.

"She's still a bit salty about you telling Abe that a man's got to fight to figure out what kind of man he is. Abe's pretty resolute about joining the Continentals as soon as he's able."

"Well, perhaps it wasn't my place," Mr. Hadley said, looking back at Abigail. "He was asking so many questions I guess I just got caught up in the moment."

"So, you don't believe every boy has that question in him?" Mercy asked.

"Well, I uh . . . I didn't say that. I said that perhaps it wasn't my place."

"Ah. . . ."

Soon everyone gathered around the fire for a meal of fish and rabbit stew. Besides Mr. Hadley, Capt. Davis and the Bells joined them for dinner. Henry gave thanks and spoke a blessing over Mercy. It seemed strange, folks making a fuss out of the change of a single year. But in this world, this birthday meant she was stepping out of childhood and into adulthood.

She didn't feel any different, but even the present company seemed to look at her differently. Even her gifts were different, this year; instead of snares, Mr. Hadley gave her a beautiful mirror, Capt. Davis a lovely shawl, and Henry and Abigail had gotten her a new dress . . . a woman's dress.

She'd known it was coming, she'd watched Adelaide's life and demeanor change. If it wasn't for the scarcity of provisions, she expected neither of them would be fishing or trapping anymore. They were ladies now, and society, no matter how rugged in the present circumstances, expected them to act like it. It'd come so fast, beginning when she'd had to step up after her mother died. She was able to slow down a little when they'd been adopted by Henry and Abigail . . . but here it was—adulthood.

She'd always looked forward to it, always tried to act older than she was, but now—now it was here, and she wasn't so sure. What if she wasn't ready? What if being an adult wasn't the dream she'd dreamed?

When the party had concluded, and everyone had gone their separate ways, Mercy sat alone with her diary by the fire taking it all in. It had been lovely, the people, the gifts, even the food with several contributions of seasoning and spice Mr. Hadley had brought from the tavern.

Everyone had seemed so excited for her, and she'd spent the day filled with excitement herself, but now it was over . . . and in a way, she couldn't help but feel like part of it had been a funeral.

"Is everything alright, dear?" Abigail asked, startling her.

"Yes, it was a wonderful celebration," Mercy smiled.

Abigail returned a soft, knowing smile.

"It was lovely." Mercy frowned. "I just feel . . . I don't know what I feel."

Abigail took a seat beside her. "I do."

"You do?"

"Mm-hmm. I remember when I was your age. My parents were fairly well off, they'd planned a grand party, there was music and dancing, there was a whole pig . . . and cider. Most of the families from church had attended, and some influential folks from town, everyone was there to celebrate the fact I was becoming a true lady.

"Sounds grand," Mercy said.

"Oh, it was a wonderful party," Abigail agreed. "But part way through the evening I realized that something had changed. I could hear it in the conversations between my mother and the other older ladies talking about my prospects with possible suitors. The way the men in the room studied me as though I was some sort of livestock they were considering. Everyone discussing my merits and shortcomings all around me, and the other young ladies . . . don't get me started on the other young ladies. Everyone planning, judging, and competing, all around me, and I realized—everything had changed."

"I know what you mean," Mercy said.

"But then my grandmother found me later and sat beside me, just like I am with you, and she told me not to listen to the hum of the gossips and busybodies around me. She told me to listen to my heart, that's where the Lord speaks to us, she said. She told me that the Lord knew the plans He had for me, and that He didn't need anyone else's advice."

"Were you scared?" Mercy asked. "And maybe sad?"

"My childhood wasn't quite as adventurous as yours, but yes. The world I saw at my celebration seemed cold, competitive, and full of expectation. The longer I thought about it, the harder it was for me to remember what it was I'd been so excited to grow up for. But then I remembered what my grandmother had told me, that the Lord had plans for me, and I felt something inside myself, like God agreed with what she'd said. And I decided right then and there that I'd follow Him wherever He'd take me, that His would be the voice that directed my path. And the fears and anxiety I'd felt about this new chapter in my story just melted away."

"Do you think He has plans for me?" Mercy asked.

"Oh, child!" Abigail squawked, placing her hand on her chest. "Haven't you seen His hand at work in your life?"

Mercy smiled sheepishly. "Yeah, I guess so."

"Mercy, the same Lord who's brought you through so many an adventure and trial, surely has wonderful plans for the rest of your story. There is a sadness when one closes a chapter, that's normal for anyone, but the Good Lord wouldn't want you to let that steal your enthusiasm for the future. Let the Lord lead your heart and take it a day at a time. Your adventures are only just beginning."

"Thank you, Mama," Mercy said, leaning her head on Abigail's shoulder. "I'm feeling better now."

"Me too," Abigail said, laying her head on Mercy's. "Oh!" Abigail gasped, sitting up.

"What is it?!"

"I think I just got kicked!" She smiled. "Here, put your hand here!"

Mercy placed her hand on Abigail's tummy and waited, holding her breath. Several moments went by as neither of them moved. Then, something bumped her hand. Mercy adjusted her palm, and it bumped it again. A broad smile crept across her face.

"Did you feel it?"

Mercy nodded slowly, concentrating, and it bumped her hand harder. "Goodness!" Mercy gasped. "It must be in a mood. Does it hurt?"

"Not at all," Abigail smiled, placing her hand where Mercy's had been. "The Lord really does have wonderful plans, doesn't He?"

In the weeks following her birthday, Mercy carried herself differently, more aware of the expectations of being a lady, while still being true to who the Lord had made her. She still let Theo ride on her shoulder, still went fishing and trapping, but when in the presence of others, she practiced thinking through her responses in conversation, being mindful of what was going on around her. She began noticing traits in women that she admired and began to mimic them in her own life.

While the other young ladies her age, including Adelaide, seemed to be fixated on nothing but prospects for marriage and romance, she found the conversations difficult to endure. In her mind she didn't have any prospects, nor did she want any, she liked her life the way it was. She was still simply grateful to have the family she had, and the war was adventure enough, she didn't want anything else.

Abigail told her the Good Lord would awaken her heart to a new adventure when it was ready, and that there was no harm in taking things slow. Like a new pair of shoes, she'd have to break in this new chapter before it would begin to feel comfortable. She just wished they could get through the war first. . . .

To Mercy's dismay, and the dismay of the rest of the Americans fighting for liberty, on November 4th, the French admiral set sail with his newly repaired fleet for the West Indies to hassle the British merchants doing business there. This left the Americans, once again, without a navy and any means of cutting off British supply and reinforcements from New York. It took every ounce of self-control to keep Mercy from sending another bucket sailing across the yard.

"Blast these infernal Frenchmen!" Capt. Davis groaned when word reached the medical tent. "Don't they have the wits to understand that without the Royal Navy the British are finished?"

"Henry says they're here to look out for the interests of France, and apparently they feel there is more benefit in the West Indies," Mercy said.

"Well, they certainly aren't making any friends here!"

"I'm sure the French admiral will be devastated to learn he has lost your affections," Mercy said.

Capt. Davis glared at her, before his features softened into a smile. "You're right. . . . What use is it to get all worked up. Let General Washington deal with it, our work remains the same."

"That's what you're always telling me."

"Aye," he nodded, returning his attention to the bandages they were rolling. "Winter will be here soon enough; I should have us preparing for that."

"Abigail says we will be going home to Cambridge for the winter, seeing the war doesn't seem to be going anywhere. Henry feels it would be better for Abigail to spend her remaining months there and deliver the baby where there are fewer obstacles to its survival."

"He's a wise man," Capt. Davis agreed. "When will you be leaving?"

"Abigail is hoping we can wait until the New Year. Henry and Benjamin are needed here so they will not be coming with us."

"War is most difficult on families. Will you be returning in the spring?"

"I—I don't know . . . Abigail says the camp is no place to raise in infant."

Capt. Davis looked up at her in surprise.

Chapter 20

It was a cold mid-November morning while Mercy and Adelaide were tending to a few early cases of the fever, that a panicking young man pulled up in a flatbed outside the tent calling for Capt. Davis. Not much had changed as far as the war was concerned, though dispatch riders had arrived telling of increased skirmishes in places like Florida and Georgia between Tory and Patriot militias. But they were far from there.

"What is it?" Capt. Davis asked, trying to calm the man down.

"Sir," the man said. "My sow, she's been in labor now for a time, and she's clearly in distress. Please, you have to come!"

"Your sow?" Capt. Davis asked skeptically.

"Yes!"

"You're a pig farmer?"

"Yes!"

"Farmers usually tend to their own stock…" Capt. Davis said, scratching his head in confusion.

"I haven't always been a farmer. … My father was a wheelwright, but that work didn't suit me. After my wife and I married last year, we moved to our own little place and bought some pigs. Pork is a mighty good living in these troubled times."

"You've never delivered piglets before?" Capt. Davis asked.

"I've never delivered anything before!" the man replied hysterically.

Capt. Davis massaged his forehead. "Mercy, would you be willing to assist me?"

"Yes, sir. What will you need?"

"My bag, and some extra rags should do it," Capt. Davis sighed.

Mercy collected his things, and they boarded the wagon. The farmer cracked the reigns, and they raced out of the camp, Mercy clinging to the buckboard for dear life. A few terrifying miles later, the farmer pulled into a humble yard belonging to a humble cabin with a humble barn.

"She's in here!" the farmer said, jumping from the buckboard and running for the lean-to off the barn.

Capt. Davis jumped down and helped Mercy to the ground. They followed the man into the lean-to where a large pink and black pig lay on its side in the straw, exhausted and distressed.

"Bring a lantern or two if you have them," Capt. Davis said, and the farmer raced out of the lean-to.

Capt. Davis set to work feeling the pig's belly, assessing its condition. "There are quite a few of them in there," he said. "Feel here, like this."

"I can feel them," Mercy said with a smile.

"Pigs usually have no trouble with the birthing process. . . ." He frowned. "But she seems to be struggling."

"What do you think it is?"

"I reckon one has turned on its side; they're supposed to come out headfirst. When they get on their side it plugs the canal, making the delivery impossible," Capt. Davis said.

"What can be done?" Mercy asked.

"I'll have to reach inside and try to turn the piglet so it's aligned quickly, if not, the mother and young will most likely die. Could you bring me some water?"

Mercy ran to the well and pulled up the pail, pouring it into a separate pail sitting on a stump and brought it over to him just as the farmer returned with the lanterns. The lanterns were hung on either side of the pig to give Capt. Davis the best lighting. He wet his hands and proceeded to check the position of the first piglet in line.

"Ah, there you are, little fella," Capt. Davis grunted. "Just as I thought. I'm going to push him further in so I can turn him."

"Have you delivered pigs before?" the farmer asked.

"I've helped deliver pigs, horses, cows, a donkey's foal, and sometimes even people," Capt. Davis grunted as he worked to turn the piglet. "The joys of being a rural doctor. Ah, there we are."

Capt. Davis removed his hand.

"Now what?" Mercy asked.

"Now we need her to push," he replied.

As if on command the sow bore down and, in a few minutes, a tiny piglet was writhing in the straw behind her.

"Awe," Mercy gasped. "It's adorable."

"There's likely nearly a dozen more where that one came from," Capt. Davis said.

"Thank you, sir," the farmer said wobbly, picking up the squirming piglet and wiping it off with a rag.

Mercy was sure she saw tears in the man's eyes.

"I thought we were going to lose her for sure," the farmer said. "She's the beginning of all our dreams."

Mercy looked back at the pig, considering his words. She'd never dreamed about having a pig . . . but then again, she hadn't really dreamed about her future much at all. It seemed funny to call a pig a dream, but if the farmer and his wife truly felt their place was farming, and the pig meant the success of that farm, then a pig really could be a dream. Henry and Abigail had dreamed about the tavern and worked hard to make it real. She decided that perhaps now was a good time to start praying and dreaming of where she was meant to be, or else how would she know it if she were to see it?

When it was all said and done, the sow had given birth to nine handsome piglets without further issues. Every one of them was different; brown with black spots, black with brown spots, pink with black spots, and some were solid colors. The farmer and his wife were elated and told Capt. Davis they'd give him one of the pigs when it came time to butcher. Mercy couldn't imagine eating one of the piglets now that'd she'd seen them, but that was the way of life. It was funny to watch the mess of them feasting on their mother's milk until their bellies were full and they fell asleep in a small heap.

"If that'll be all, I think we'd best get back to our other patients," Capt. Davis said.

The farmer nodded, and they all climbed back onto the buckboard. After they were situated, he snapped the reigns and they were off, only this time Mercy didn't have to cling to her seat.

When they arrived back at camp, Capt. Davis thanked him for their safe return and held out his hand.

The farmer shook it. "The name's Miles, and I thank ya kindly."

"Tobias, and you're very welcome," Capt. Davis said.

The two of them waved as the farmer pulled away. "Tobias?" Mercy asked with a smile.

"Yes, that's my name," Capt. Davis replied, with a puzzled expression. "What did you think it was—Captain?"

"No," Mercy snorted. "Maybe . . . Percival?"

"You're kidding," he chuffed.

"I am," Mercy smiled. "Hmm, Tobias . . . Tobias."

"Yes?"

She studied his features, looking him up and down while she walked a circle around him. "I suppose it'll have to do," she sighed with a shrug. "There's no changing it now."

"What's wrong with my name?" he asked.

"Nothing—I just knew it'd get a rise out of you."

Capt. Davis rolled his eyes. "Come on, we've got patients to attend to."

Mercy followed him back into the tent grinning as she went. *Tobias.* The name actually fit him quite well, it was a handsome and strong name, yet it was soft all the same. She marveled that she'd known him so long without ever hearing it—the price of living in a military camp.

"Do you think anyone has ever had a pig as a pet?" Mercy asked as they worked.

"No," he scoffed. "Did you not see what those things grow up to be?"

"But the little ones are incredibly adorable, when I held them, my heart melted."

"They're food. Don't you like bacon?"

"Of course I like bacon, everyone likes bacon. I've just never seen bacon look like that before. . . ."

He looked at her, shaking his head.

"Bacon—that'd be an adorable name for a piglet."

"Prophetic, to say the least," he mused, checking a patient's wound. "Perhaps your destiny is to be a farmer who raises animals including owls and then doesn't sell or eat them."

"How would that work?" Mercy asked enthusiastically.

"It wouldn't," he answered dryly. "You'd starve to death while your creatures ate up all your food."

"Maybe your name really is Captain," Mercy said. "Captain Killjoy."

"Ahh, those who can't debate, debase," Capt. Davis sighed.

"You're insufferable."

"I know, it's dreadful. At times I even keep my own self up at night. . . ."

Mercy snorted.

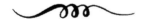

Later that evening, when everyone had returned to the wagons for dinner, Mercy shared the story about the piglets and her desire to have one as a pet.

"I had a piglet as a pet once," Jonathan Bell said. "I hid it from my pa for as long as I could."

"I remember that," Mrs. Bell said.

"What happened?" Mercy asked.

"I kept the piglet in the woods a ways back from our house," Jonathan continued. "I'd bring him scraps of food from my dinner; most of the time he ate better than I did."

"This was back when he wasn't but seven or eight," Mrs. Bell said.

"He grew fast and demanding," Jonathan chuffed. "That was his undoing, I'm afraid. I'd hid him for a couple of months, but one day I couldn't get out to him as early as I usually did, and he started putting up a fuss. I remember I could hear it through the cabin walls, and I prayed my pa would think it was just the wind whistling. But . . . as fate would have it, Pa had work outside to do, and sure enough he heard my pig squealing away."

"Oh no!" Mercy gasped.

"Yup. I remember watching him set off into the woods to find him. I was shakin' so bad knowing I was about to get the switch and I had no idea what was going to become of my pig. It wasn't but a few moments and I saw him coming back through the woods leading my pig on a rope."

"Then what happened?" Abe asked.

"Well, Pa knew it'd been me since I was shakin' so bad. Mama came outside with her hands on her hips, and I figured when Pa was done with me, she was probably fixin' to skin me alive."

"Oh, good heavens," Mrs. Bell chuffed, rolling her eyes.

"Pa knelt in front of me, looking me dead in the eyes, and asked if it was my pig. I nodded. He asked me how long I'd been hiding him, and when I told him he actually seemed impressed. He'd asked where I got him, and I told him I'd found him wandering the woods . . . which was true. Pa said he must have escaped from one of the farms nearby and we had an obligation to return him."

"Did he whoop ya?" asked David.

"No," Mrs. Bell interjected. "The poor boy was so broken hearted he could hardly stand for all his sobbing."

"We found that our nearest neighbor's sow had passed suddenly when the piglets were a few weeks old. A few of them, without their mother to keep them, had squirted through the pen and he'd given them up as dead. He thanked me for keeping his pig alive and gave me a coin for the trouble. I cried the whole way home," Jonathan concluded.

"What became of the pig?" Abe asked.

"It went the way of all pigs, I suppose," Mrs. Bell said.

"Was it a good pet while you had it?" Mercy asked.

"Surprisingly, yes," Jonathan replied. "It behaved much like a dog and would follow me everywhere while I played in the woods."

"I knew it," Mercy said triumphantly.

"We are *not* adding a pig," Abigail chided. "An owl is plenty."

Chapter 21

The seasons had changed so subtly during the past transformative month of Mercy's life that she'd hardly realized the change had taken place; that is, until she found herself trembling as she cracked the thin layer of ice off the top of the water barrel. November was at its end, winter preparations were nearly complete in the camp, and the war was fixing to hibernate for another season.

It wasn't the cold that bothered her so much as the wind that drove it. A cold still morning could easily be endured as her many layers and wool stockings could keep it at bay, but this wind . . . It pierced through her layered armor and drove the cold into her bones. Her toes stung and her fingers tingled as she collected precious water for her patients.

Carefully carrying the pail into the town hall-turned-field hospital, a warm wave enveloped her, courtesy of the fireplace that softly crackled a few feet inside. It was a tremendous blessing to be quartered in a building this time of year, and it would surely mean the difference between life and death, at least for a few.

"Have you heard the news?" Capt. Davis asked, taking the pail and setting it down for her.

"What news?"

"Our spies say that just yesterday a fleet of British ships carrying several thousand redcoats set sail from New York."

"What do you think it means?" Mercy asked.

"I'm not sure, but our officers believe they're either evacuating or sailing to the West Indies to confront the French. Either way the redcoats no longer see their effectiveness here is a victory. We've held them for a year, even without the French navy; surely the king has seen that British success is no longer feasible and is preparing to cut his losses. I think I'm ready to allow myself the pleasure of believing the war is in its final breaths."

"It hardly seems possible," Mercy smiled.

"Of course, once the redcoats are gone, we'll still have the Tories to contend with. I expect there will be many upheavals in the months following the war as we settle our differences with our families and neighbors."

"Like your father?"

"Aye. . . . He's a proud man. He will not take our victory without insult. Nor will he see my choosing the side that won something to boast of."

"He seems like a difficult man to please," Mercy said.

"Impossible. The only way for me to please him would be for me to be him," Capt. Davis sighed.

"Maybe after the war he'll come to see things differently."

"If only."

Mercy set out amongst their patients; there were only a couple dozen so far. Conditions in the camp were constantly improving, the benefits of staying in one place long enough to transform it. Fever and dysentery were a constant enemy still far more fatal than the redcoats. The random foraging skirmishes provided the occasional wounded soldier often enough to keep things from getting mundane. All their losses seemed sad and foolish with the war so near its end.

Abigail had been kept from working in the hospital to prevent her from catching the fever in her current state, so she worked with Mrs. Bell teaching in the camp school. The baby was growing, as was Abigail, and as she grew, so did the anticipation of the new person who'd soon be joining them. Mercy would smile to herself as she wrote in her diary while Henry and Abigail haggled about baby names by the fire. Only a few more months now.

The fighting season had passed so quietly compared to the prior year that, had they not lived in the camp, one could almost forget there was a war going on at all. It was entirely possible the king had already called an end to the war and the orders simply hadn't arrived on their shores yet. Henry said it took months for word to travel back and forth across the ocean.

When she'd finished with her patients, Mercy and Adelaide took their leave and returned to the wagons. Arriving a little after noon, Mercy was delighted to find Henry and Benjamin back early from their foraging mission; sitting wrapped in wool blankets near the fire to thaw out.

"Did you find anything?" Mercy asked.

"Aye," Henry smiled. "Our party was able to harvest a few deer feeding on leftovers in the farmers' fields."

"See any redcoats?" Adelaide asked.

"No," Ben answered. "We were hunting west of here; it'd be more likely we'd run into Tories or Indians."

"Did you hear about the redcoats sailing out of New York?" Mercy asked.

"Aye, it looks as though they may be pulling out. Washington will need his spies now more than ever," Henry said.

"How come?" Abigail asked.

"We want them to surrender, not just leave," Henry said. "When their numbers get low enough to give us a significant advantage, we need to take them before they can escape back to England."

"Why?" asked Mercy.

"So we can set the terms of their surrender and the end of the war."

"What does that mean?" Ben asked.

"Terms of Surrender are like a binding contract between the participants of the conflict. If the redcoats just leave, they can choose not to recognize us as our own sovereign nation, which affects our political position as far as nations of the world are concerned. Without an official surrender, they could still claim us as colonies of England and continue to prop up the Tories, leading to a destructive never-ending civil war. But, if they surrender, we can present the terms of their surrender, first on the list being our sovereignty; second, they are in no way able to aid the Tories either monetarily or militarily; third, all prisoners of war are to be returned immediately, and so on."

"So, if they were to just leave, they wouldn't be bound to do any of those things?" Mercy asked.

"That's correct. Following their surrender, a treaty would need to be arranged, laying out the ground rules for relations between our two nations for the foreseeable future concerning trade and the like. Congress will have their hands full for quite some time before the matter is finally concluded," Henry said.

"And then what?" Mercy asked.

"Then, we'll have to learn how to be our own nation," Henry sighed. "Everything will have to be made new, governments, laws, currency. England is woven into every fiber of our society; when she's gone, we'll finally understand just how much work there is to be done."

"Well, work or no work, I'm ready for it all to be over," Abigail said. "We've achieved victory, we're just waiting for the final word. It'd be a blessing if it'd come before the new year, then all these poor boys could go home before the *dreadful* cold sets in."

"Aye, we should pray for it," Henry agreed.

"With the war ending, I suppose there are other things we'll have to plan as well," Abigail said, motioning to where Adelaide sat beside Ben.

Adelaide blushed, as she looked dreamily into his eyes.

Ben cleared his throat. "Well, um, I'd have to have a trade first . . . and a place of my own. I don't really have either," he said, looking down at his shoes.

"Nonsense," Abigail said. "You've learned many skills while serving in the army, and Henry and I would surely help you get started. Why, we could help you open your own tavern . . . we've already built one once. Right, Henry?"

"She's right," Henry said. "You don't have to go it alone, you have a family, son."

Benjamin nodded.

Watching Adelaide beam at the thought of it brought a smile to Mercy's face. It was like watching one of the stories she'd read. Her best friend and her big brother, like it was meant to be. Everything was as it was meant to be.

Abe and David returned from school, wood was added to the fire, and everyone sat down to a dinner of bread and roast venison. For what seemed like the first time in years, the dinner conversation didn't revolve around the war. Henry and Abigail shared their baby names debate; Henry wanted to name a baby boy Henry, but Abigail didn't want to spend the rest of her life hollering "Henry," hoping for the one but getting the other. Abigail liked the name Asher from the Bible, but Henry had never met anyone by that name, and he felt folks would think he was some sort of ash collector.

After a while, David piped up and offered his name as a good solution since neither side seemed to be gaining any ground and naming the baby David would secure both goals, two people in the family would have the same name, and David was a good king from the Bible. That notion got everyone laughing, except David of course who seemed to be quite fond of his idea.

Then they got started on the girl names. Abigail liked Mary, while Henry liked Beth. Both sounded fine to Mercy, though she doubted you could know exactly who a person was before you met them. The debate went round and round with each member having their say in the matter, but the results were so divided that by the time they went to bed nothing had been decided. She loved her family.

That night Mercy had to stifle laughter as she wrote the whole evening down in her diary. They were all of them delightfully silly in their own way.

Chapter 22

December 25th, Christmas morning, found Mercy warming herself by the fire in the hospital. The room smelled of pine, a wreath hung above the fireplace, garlands of ivy, laurel, and holly were hung about the room to brighten the atmosphere. A kettle of warm cider hung near the fire, and a few flakes of snow fell outside the windows.

There would be a party at the Oak Haven Tavern that evening; Mercy wished Adelaide could attend, but the Puritans had their own way. There would be fiddling, dancing, plumb pudding, cider, ham, and candies. Everyone would spend the evening in merriment, celebrating the birth of the Lord.

"There's little work to be done here, I'm surprised you're not over at the tavern with your family preparing for the celebration,"

Capt. Davis said, pouring a mug of cider and handing it to her, before pouring his own.

"Thank you," Mercy smiled, holding the warm mug in her hands, inhaling deeply the sweet spicy smell of the cider. "I spend nearly every free moment surrounded by my family. Incredible as they are, sometimes I need a little break."

"I can understand that," Capt. Davis said, taking a sip. "It's an honor to know you don't feel the need to take a break from me."

"Why do you think I leave at the end of each day?" Mercy teased.

Capt. Davis frowned.

"Just this morning David gifted Abe a sailing ship he'd constructed using branches and twine, a masterful work for a boy his age . . . it wasn't until Abe put on his linen shirt that he figured out where the sails had come from," Mercy said.

Capt. Davis choked on his cider. "I imagine Abigail wasn't too pleased about that."

"She's soft on boys," Mercy sighed. "She just told Abe they'd get him another one, and that it was a good thing David had had the sense to choose his most worn garment."

"She has the heart of a saint," Capt. Davis said.

"Last week he tried to make a fireplace in the wagon from a broken clay pitcher and set the wagon on fire. It was a good thing Henry and Ben were on their way back from the parade field;

there was little damage done. I thought Henry would be furious, but he simply told David that his notion was a good one but needed some modifications and more practical testing."

"I do remember hearing about that," Capt. Davis said. "Creative minds are what propel our society forward."

"With David at the helm, we're likely to be propelled right off a cliff," Mercy mused.

"Abraham seems to have grown up in the past year."

"Yes, I think the absence of Henry and Ben has awoken a duty in him that compels him to take up their slack."

"It's incredible the growth one can achieve if given the opportunity," Capt. Davis said.

"But the heart has to be willing to seize the opportunity, otherwise nothing changes. While working in the tavern, I saw many folks despise the opportunities given them, only to spend the evening drowning their disappointments in their cups, blaming the world rather than themselves for the things that could have been if they'd only put in the effort."

"Have you always been so incredibly perceptive?" Capt. Davis marveled.

"When my mama died, I wanted to help Papa, but to do that I had to learn to do the things Mama had done. So, I trained myself to observe the other women around me, to pay attention and practice the things they were doing, and the rest I had to learn from making mistakes, just like we do here."

"The power of perceptive observation is one of the finest disciplines of wisdom. A fool sees but doesn't perceive, but to the wise, seeing is not satisfied until we understand."

"Like the way you study the grotesque nature of our work so closely."

"Aye. If I can understand it, maybe I can fix it. Everyone has troubles that stand in the way of our dreams. We can either drown them in our cups or rise and rise again until we overcome them. Either way, we only get one shot at this life, and we'll have to live with the consequences."

"That's why we're fighting, to take that one shot at a life lived in freedom," Mercy sighed.

"Aye, and we'll have it." He smiled. "To think that we are amongst the fortunate few who will be here to see it."

Later that evening, everyone gathered at the tavern. Piano music was accompanied by a fiddle as young officers danced with the eligible ladies, older officers discussed military matters and politics, and the older women judged and gossiped about every young couple in the room. Abigail and Henry volunteered to help the tavern owners in serving, Benjamin had opted out of the whole affair, choosing to spend his time with Adelaide that evening. Mercy, who'd never been a guest at a ball or anything of the like, found a chair in a quiet corner from where she could take it all in.

The atmosphere was uncomfortably warm with the heavy din of conversation spoiling the pleasure of the musical concert in her opinion. The air was filled with smells of cider, ham, pipe smoke, and pine. The sight of couples, men in fine uniforms, and ladies in their best dresses, twirling about in synchronized fashion was mesmerizing.

"Excuse me, Miss Young, may I have the pleasure of this next dance?"

Her heart skipped a beat as she looked up to see Capt. Davis looking dapper in his dress uniform, offering her a gloved hand.

"I—" she stammered, looking for Abigail. "I—uh . . . don't know how to dance," she whispered.

"That's alright, everyone has a first dance. I'll lead and you just follow."

Mercy glanced to the sideline and caught Abigail's eye. A smile spread across Abigail's face, and she nodded to Mercy, gesturing with her hands for Mercy to get up. Mercy looked back at the gloved hand that hovered patiently, awaiting her reply. Slowly she reached out trembling fingers and took it.

Gently, Capt. Davis lifted her from her chair and guided her out onto the floor. Her whole body shook, and she felt as if every eye in the room was on her. Stifling heat caused sweat to roll past her temple and into her ear. She watched the other couples and held his hand as she saw the other ladies do. The music started, and she moved. . . .

"Very good," Capt. Davis whispered. "Now you are going to twirl to your right around the lady to your right and come back to me."

Mercy did her best to copy the other ladies and found him again.

"Excellent."

Mercy glanced towards the gaggles of older ladies fanning themselves and whispering assertively to one another as they watched the spectacle.

"Don't let the old hens distract you," he whispered, drawing her gaze back to him. "Their only joy in life is to play matchmaker and relive the glory days of the romance they once had. Most of them are actually quite miserable."

Mercy nodded, trying to concentrate on her next movement.

"You're learning fast, from here on it's simply repetition until the song is finished. Then all the men bow, the ladies curtsy, and we all clap for the musicians."

Mercy nodded again, her muscles beginning to relax. She twirled around, found him again, a couple steps left, a couple steps right, another twirl. And she looked up, into his eyes, and they looked back at her with warm admiration, held her there in a way they never had before. The thing was so distracting that she misstepped, tripping on his foot, but he caught her, and as she looked around, it seemed no one had noticed.

She searched his eyes again, trying to understand what she'd seen, and there it was. He wasn't looking at her, he was looking . . . into her. She wanted to say something to break the awkward trance, but it was time to twirl again. When they came back together, the music stopped. The men bowed, the ladies curtsied, everyone clapped.

He let her hand slip from his. Smiling, he moved as if to speak . . .

"Attention!" A gruff officer called the room to order, and everyone fell silent. Capt. Davis released her from his gaze, and following orders, directed his attention to the front.

The officer kneaded a piece of parchment between thick fingers as he searched for the words to say.

"My fellow gentlemen and ladies," he began. "I do not know if I've ever been handed a more difficult assignment." He searched the room with sorrowful eyes. "We've all endured hardships the likes of which no mortal should ever have to, and we've endured them past the measure of our endurance and still, we have risen to the call for so many a year."

He looked back to the letter, considering his next words.

"It appears all the indications and hopes of nearing final victory have been a deception."

Gasps and murmurs rose across the room.

"The fleet of British ships and soldiers which sailed from New York a month past did not sail for England, nor the West Indies as we so hopefully supposed. A dispatch rider has only just delivered this unfitting news after riding day and night for two days without rest. The fleet which left New York—" A deep breath. "Has appeared off the shores of Savannah, Georgia only two mornings ago."

More gasps filled the room.

"The Patriots in Georgia, though a gritty lot, will be no match for such an invasion, and the distance is too great for us to reach them in time. The redcoats, it seems, have adjusted their strategy. Having been beaten in the north, they've set their sights on the wealth of the south, intending to rip our fragile union in two."

"Never!" yelled a young officer.

"Indeed, never!" agreed the speaker. "We've only just received this news. We will revise our strategy, and we will beat them in the south as well . . . No matter how long it takes. May God grant us His grace!"

"Where are the French?" yelled another officer.

"Our allies are otherwise occupied," the older officer replied. "But this is not their war, it's ours. This is all the information we have at present. Our thoughts and prayers should turn to those brave few who will face our foe amongst their farms and families until we can organize ourselves and come to their aid. I regret that such news must come during a well-deserved celebration."

The officer bowed humbly and made his way out of the tavern with several other generals following close behind him.

The room watched them leave in stunned silence before a chorus of shock and protest replaced the cheerful atmosphere. Mercy's mind reeled in disbelief. . . . They'd had them—had the redcoats cornered—the war was almost over. It didn't make any sense. . . . They'd met the enemy, they'd fought, suffered, endured, and now it was time for it to be over.

But they'd slipped away, just like General Washington had done so many times before. Is this how General Howe had felt? Having a sure victory time and time again only to have it slip away? It felt . . . like someone had knocked all the air out of her. Like being stuck in a horrible nightmare she couldn't wake from, it just repeated itself over and over in blood and brokenness and loss.

"Are you alright?" Capt. Davis asked. Then he shook his head. "Of course you're not. How could any of us be alright?"

"What will we do?" Mercy asked.

"That's what those generals left to figure out. They'll be in the war council all night, I'm sure. We can't simply march the whole army south, or the Brits will simply retake the north. They've wisely divided us."

"Could you for once, stop praising them!" Mercy pleaded.

"I'm sorry it upsets you, but to understand it, we must be able to acknowledge when one has done well, even if it is our enemy.

General Clinton has retaken control of the war. If General Washington sends too many men south, General Clinton will march out of New York, and we'll be in a bind to corner him again. If we don't march enough men south, we may very well loose it. The redcoats probably hope to find more support in the southern colonies; Tories are thick as thieves down there."

"But doesn't this news bother you?!" Mercy asked.

"It may work together for good." Capt. Davis shrugged. "With so many Tories in the south, we'd probably have to have it out with them if we'd won the war at any rate. Perhaps this way we can face them as subjects of the crown and embrace them as brothers once they've been defeated. Then the war can truly be over."

"You're saying we'll win?" Mercy asked in surprise.

"If we win," Capt. Davis corrected. "And for that I believe we must reconcile our differences with the French. The king's Achillies heel is his dependance on the sea."

"Argh," Mercy held her head. "Worst Christmas ever. . . ."

"Yes, I suppose it is. . . ." Capt. Davis frowned in disappointment.

Despite everyone's best efforts, the evening was ruined beyond repair. Shattered hopes gave way to frustration, which then turned into resolve. The Americans had already come this far, they weren't about to let the king's shrewd maneuver rob them of their freedom. The outcome would be liberty or death.

That night, Mercy angrily flipped through pages of hopeful entries in her diary. The king had made a fool of her, of all of them. Through grit teeth she began to write her Christmas entry, the quill scratching on the page in bitter strokes. She wanted simply to rip the pages of the past months out, but it wouldn't change what was. What *was* sure, was that every time the war took a dramatic turn, so did her life. The question was, how was it going to change this time?

Chapter 23

On December 29th, Mercy found herself packing up their wagon for the long ride back to Cambridge with a heavy heart. The redcoats' invasion of the south still had everyone reeling, and Mercy wouldn't be here to see it sorted out. Abigail was far along now, and she needed Mercy's help often. It was wise to send her away from the fever in the camp, but Mercy knew they'd be gone for a long time. There was no guarantee they'd be coming back at all.

It seemed funny; the wagon was taking them home, but Mercy couldn't help feeling like they were leaving it. Henry and Benjamin prepared the team but wouldn't be coming along this time. Their unit was needed to scout the redcoats and make sure General Clinton wasn't planning something in the north.

Jonathan Bell was given leave to escort the two families back safely.

When they'd finished their preparations, Mercy wandered over to the hospital to bid Capt. Davis farewell. She hated leaving him at the height of fever season, but without Henry, Abigail would need her in Cambridge.

Entering, she found him at a desk pouring over his journals, no doubt comparing notes between past and present cases. He looked up from his notes and smiled at her, although be it somewhat forced, before standing to greet her.

"I assume you are all ready to go?" he asked, with a quick bow.

"Yes, we've just finished."

"Ah, that's good. You'll need to take good care of Abigail; the last months can be quite challenging."

"Yes, I'll do that," Mercy replied. "Will you be alright without me?"

"We'll have to manage," he replied. "Though . . . I won't be here for much longer."

Mercy looked at him, puzzled.

"I've requested a transfer," he said, fiddling with his cuff.

"What?!"

"My duty is to those who are doing the fighting . . . a blacksmith could tend to things here. The war has moved to the southern colonies, and I've requested a transfer to serve those who'll be fighting desperately against the invasion."

"But you heard the general, they don't stand a chance against a force that large. . . ."

"All the more reason I should leave without delay," he said.

"But Henry and Benjamin are here; I can't go to the south . . . what will happen when I return to camp?!"

"There will be another surgeon who will take my place. I've already drafted letters instructing him of your qualifications and the asset you and Adelaide are to the cause here."

Mercy's mind spun. What was he saying? "You won't be here when I return?"

"No."

She took a step away from him. Why did she feel as though he was abandoning her? What he was saying made sense, they surely could use him in the conflict . . . but somewhere in her it didn't make sense.

He stepped towards her. "Mercy."

And she took another step back, clenching her jaw against the fog in her mind, she glared at him through tear-filling eyes.

He stopped. "I'm sorry," he said, looking into her as he had during the dance, albeit mournfully.

It was too much, everything was changing too fast, first the baby, then the war, and now Capt. Davis? Panic seized her, it was suffocating, as if she was sinking into a turbulent sea of uncertainty. Turning from him, she dashed out of the hospital before she could be completely undone.

By the time she reached the wagon, her tears had overflowed her capacity to contain them. She stormed by everyone saying their goodbyes and clawed her way into the back of the wagon. "Let's go!" she half choked half growled.

She wrapped her arms around her head to block out the curious murmurs and buried her head in her lap. In a few moments she felt the wagon rocking as the passengers boarded. Abigail sat beside her and laid her palm on Mercy's back. She wanted to run away, but there was nowhere to go, and there wouldn't be, not for a week.

The reigns snapped, the wagon began rolling, and Mercy remained buried. Why was God constantly tearing her world apart? She didn't ask for much, she was content with what little they'd had. . . . Why was it suddenly all gone again? Something inside, a Comforter, brought to her remembrance all the Bible characters who'd gone through terrible and difficult things; Daniel and his friends, Joseph, Moses, and the prophets all seemed to have it really bad.

But God had never abandoned them, and in the end their purpose had been greater than anything they could have imagined. If they'd given up when things got hard, no one would ever have known they existed. It had been their character in the fire, that had changed the world.

The notion did nothing to lessen the fire she found herself in, but she felt a peace in knowing that, even now, God had plans for her, for all of them. In that peace, and exhaustion, Mercy allowed the wagon to rock her to sleep.

It was late afternoon by the time she woke. Her feet were numb with the cold and her back ached from the position she'd slept in. Though it wasn't late, the days were short this time of year and Abe had followed Jonathan's lead and led the team off the road to make camp for the evening.

"My, that was a good long rest," Abigail said as Mercy sat up. "I doubt you'll do much sleeping tonight."

Mercy gave a halfhearted smile.

"Come along then, let's get some supper cooking."

Mercy climbed painfully from the wagon and made her way over to a fire ring which had been used by many travelers in the past. The boys set about collecting firewood while Jonathan and Nathaniel took care of the horses.

"Are you feeling better?" Abigail asked.

"Maybe?" Mercy groaned. "It hasn't been an easy week."

"Not for any of us."

"Did you know Capt. Davis was transferring south?" Mercy asked.

Abigail hesitated. "I didn't know before yesterday when he came to talk to Henry."

"What did he want to talk to Henry about?" Mercy asked, in surprise.

"I would've thought he'd have told you?" Abigail said.

Mercy broke some twigs and added them to the small fire Abe had started. "I kind of ran out on him while he was talking. . . ." Mercy mumbled.

"You what?! Goodness, Mercy, your poor emotions surely are a tempest."

"I don't know, I was angry! . . .and sad," she said, throwing up her hands. "He's always been there, and—and I don't like when things change. Not this much change. Who will I talk to while I work? Who will teach me? Who will get under my skin, and then laugh when I correct them. Who will listen to my complaining and then disregard it all with sarcastic logic? Who will listen to me . . ." Mercy choked.

"Perhaps that's why he asked Henry's permission to write you," Abigail said, lifting her chin.

"He what?"

"Maybe he doesn't know how he'll carry on without you either."

"Why would he need permission? I've written to him before."

"Yes, but you're not that little girl anymore, Mercy."

"Oh . . . *Oh!*" Mercy's eyes widened.

Abigail smiled.

A new confusion washed over her. What did it mean? He was probably just being proper . . . wasn't he? They were friends, he was like an older brother . . . a charming, handsome, dancing kind of older brother. Right?

"Why did he ask to be reassigned?" Mercy asked.

"You know why, Mercy. He's a man of principle, and his principles demanded he go where he was needed the most. He couldn't rest knowing there were boys suffering without his care anymore than you could, you know that."

Mercy nodded. Abigail was right, the soldiers in the south needed him more than she did, and it'd be wrong for him not to go. The whole thing stirred up emotions and feelings she didn't even know she had, and she needed time to work through them.

"I saw the two of you dance." Abigail smiled, adding some bacon to the frypan.

"I was so nervous I don't hardly remember it," Mercy confessed. "Especially with that awful announcement. . . . Mercy blushed. "I hadn't expected to be dancing."

"You were the handsomest pair on the floor," Abigail said.

Mercy scoffed, trying to hide her smile.

"You're young, Mercy. Let it work itself out without making too many judgments too early. The purest things in life take a little time and testing; the Good Lord knows what He's doing."

"He may not even write after the way I behaved." Mercy shrugged.

"He'll write."

In the following days, Mercy's heart was as tossed about as she was on the road to Cambridge. It was as if someone had blown the candle out and no matter how hard she tried to look into the future, nothing was clear. Even her relationships seemed to lack definition. If this is what it was to be an adult, she was not prepared for it. Perhaps some time away from it all in Cambridge was just what she needed.

When they arrived at the tavern, Mrs. Hadley chased them all in out of the cold. Mr. Hadley had spent the last few months building a separate cabin behind the tavern for himself and Mrs. Hadley so Abigail and the Youngs could have the main house. Mercy and Abigail would share the main bedroom, while the boys stayed upstairs. Mrs. Hadley demanded Theo stay in Mr. Hadley's old lean-to off the barn.

Mercy's spirits relaxed the moment the familiarity and warmth of the tavern wrapped her in its embrace. She was glad to aid in the kitchen and put her hands to work on something other than her patients. The tavern was always busy during the winter months. With all the cold and snow, folks had nothing better to do than pass the time chatting with their neighbors over a mug of ale.

As the weeks passed, the routine of cooking, serving, and cleaning soon replaced the routine she'd had in the camp. Her brothers worked with Mr. Hadley tending to the chores and keeping the fires burning. Mrs. Hadley and Abigail would sit peeling potatoes talking about Benjamin and Adelaide, and from time-to-time Mercy's tingling ears would hear her own name come up.

And thus, as January gave way to February, her life took on a new pattern of work in the tavern, trapping in the woods, and waiting. Waiting for the baby, waiting for spring, waiting for a letter that never came. Every time the postrider arrived, Mercy would wait with bated breath as Abigail sorted the mail, but so far, the letters had all been for Abigail.

Chapter 24

February 6, 1779

My Dear Friend,

I pray you will forgive me for being so long in writing this letter, it took far longer than I had expected to find my place and settle in. While I feel no shame in my decision to redeploy myself where my services to my countrymen are most profitable, I've felt nothing but shame for the way I in which I carelessly relayed my decision to you. I must confess, I did not fully understand your reasons for receiving the news with such anguish, but I believe I understand them now.

These past weeks have been some of the loneliest of my life and it has not been for lack of work or aides. There is an emptiness in the medical tent, and my life, that I'd anticipated, but gravely miscalculated in depth. I hadn't realized that your friendship had become very much like a home to me these past difficult years, and I'd not wanted to give it the credit it was due for fear of what it may mean, or worse, that I might lose it. I'm regrettably sorry, Mercy, and I pray your forgiveness. My dishonesty regarding your worth was only a cowardly defense of myself, not wanting to subject myself to the pain of emptiness I now know fully, and you endured from the moment you heard of my departure.

I didn't realize how much light you cast into this dark and difficult world; into my world. Perhaps I was too busy to notice, or perhaps I didn't want to acknowledge it. You were only a child when we met on Dorchester Heights, and I think my mind, for propriety's sake, tried to keep you that way. It appears that for all my imagined intellect, my heart is wiser and more sincere. You are a far greater friend, and dearer to me, than any I've ever had. I pray my carelessness hasn't cost me your affection.

As you've probably already received word, the redcoats took Savannah on the 29th. We lost nearly the entire garrison: killed or captured. General Lord Cornwallis seems to be a tenacious foe, and he intends to use his advantage for as long as he has it. He's already added Augusta to his conquest just this week. We are outmatched at nearly every engagement, though I've heard General Moultrie was able to miraculously defeat a superior mixed force at Port Royal, South Carolina on the 3rd. God be praised.

There is no winter in the south, or not so much as to cause a break in the conflict. I find myself nearly dizzy with the constant flow of new patients. The southern conflict is fierce and active, reminding me *of the difficult time we all faced in 1777. I wonder if the casualties could possibly have been greater if we'd have fought the redcoats street by street in New York when we had the chance. The Lord only knows.*

There is something awe inspiring about the people of this fledging nation; even in the face of so many defeats, both in the north and south, we are not wanting for those who will rise up and fight. Regardless of the outcome, I am proud to be an American. I will serve for as long as the Good Lord sees fit to put breath in my lungs, and should I perish, it will not be in regret.

I eagerly await the light and warmth of your reply, whatever it may be.

Your friend, and fellow servant of the cause,

Tobias Davis.

"Took it six days in getting here," Abigail mused.

"Well, what do you think?" Mercy asked anxiously, as Abigail finished reading.

Abigail studied the letter. "I don't feel he's being very cryptic, dear."

"I know . . . just, tell me what you think he's saying."

Abigail looked at the letter again. "Well, it looks like the redcoats are giving us a hard time in the south, and he has his hands full."

"Not, *that* part . . ." Mercy groaned.

Abigail laughed, giving Mercy a gentle nudge. "I think he's saying that being absent from you has caused him to realize things his heart understood but hadn't yet reached that calculating mind of his."

"What things?" Mercy asked.

"Goodness, Mercy!" Abigail chuffed. "It's all there in black and white."

Mercy looked at her, pleading.

"Alright, I think . . . *just* like he said, that you were a bigger part of his life than he allowed himself to realize, and now that you aren't there, it's all he can see."

"He makes it sound like I should be a little salty—should I be?" Mercy asked indignantly. "I mean, according to him, he hardly even realized I was there before he left."

"Is that what you read?!" Abigail guffawed, holding up the letter. "You never miss an opportunity to hold a person at your mercy, do you?"

Mercy smiled wryly. "I've learned a lot from this war."

Abigail burst out laughing, holding her hands on her chest. "Oh, Dear Lord, please help this poor young man! He's practically pleading with you, Mercy!"

"I suppose he does sound a *bit* repentant," Mercy agreed. "Though he did—how did he put it? Oh, here it is, 'act cowardly,' and cause me 'anguish.'"

"But he's apologized," Abigail said. "And he seems sincere."

Mercy sighed. "I guess only time will tell if he has truly amended his character."

Abigail shook her head. "You know he's as fine a ma—" She gasped.

"What is it?!" Mercy asked.

"I—I don't know. I think the baby is coming," Abigail said, wide eyed.

"Now?!"

"Yes, now! Quick, fetch Mrs. Hadley!"

Mercy burst from the bedroom, through the kitchen, and out into the cold night air. She forgot about her stocking feet until the melting snow soaked through to her toes. She stopped momentarily before deciding it was already too late and continuing on. Reaching the cabin, she slid to a stop atop the muddied planking outside the door.

"Mrs. Hadley! Mrs. Hadley!" She banged on the door.

There was a scuffling of shoes inside the cabin and the door creaked open. "What is it, Mercy?" the older woman asked.

"It's Mama," Mercy gasped. "She says the baby's coming!"

"Oh! Goodness, they do seem to favor the night, don't they! Mr. Hadley!" she called. "We've got a baby coming! Fetch the boys, I'm gonna need water, hot and cold, a wash basin, and some spare towels. Mercy, you come with me, I'll need an assistant!"

Mrs. Hadley threw on her cloak and set off across the yard, with Mercy at her heels. Reaching the tavern, Mrs. Hadley bustled through the kitchen and into the bedroom.

"How are we, Abigail?" she asked.

"It's started," Abigail said. "I can feel things tightening in regular intervals."

"I've got the men tending to the fire and water; this is your first time, it'll be a little while yet," Mrs. Hadley smiled, patting Abigail on the hand.

Mercy felt a fear creep over her. She knew plenty of women who'd died during or after giving birth. Her own mother had gotten sick and never fully recovered before the fever took her. She wanted to be excited, wanted to believe that everything was going to be okay, but she knew this would be the most dangerous test Abigail would ever undergo.

"Mercy? Are you alright?" Abigail asked.

"I'm praying, Mama," Mercy said, trying to hold her emotions in check.

"Thank you," Abigail smiled. "I'm a bit anxious myself. I know you're worried, and I know you have every reason to be. But the Lord hasn't spent these past years making me strong for nothing, nor do I believe he would be so good as to give me a miracle child only to take it from me. But whatever happens, I know He's good, and this life of ours is limited from the day we enter the world. We have another home, and a glorious life awaiting us, so in life or death, we can rejoice."

"I know that, Mama." Mercy bit her lip, fighting back tears. "But I've already got one mama waiting for me . . . I need a mama here too."

"Come here, Mercy," Abigail said, patting the bed beside her.

Mercy obeyed and Abigail pulled her in close so Mercy's head rested on her shoulder.

"Whenever I count my blessings, I always count you twice," Abigail whispered, planting a kiss on her head.

Mercy closed her eyes, releasing a single tear to roll its way down her cheek. "I count you a thousand times," Mercy choked.

The next few hours passed as Abigail's condition intensified. Mr. Hadley brought water and kept a kettle going while playing Draughts with the boys. Abigail did her best to put on a brave face, but she couldn't hide the shortness of breath or the involuntary contortions of her face. Mrs. Hadley assured her that everything was coming along just fine.

Mercy dabbed her forehead with a damp rag, praying unceasingly in her mind.

"We're close now," Mrs. Hadley said with a confident smile. "Alright, Abigail, it's time to work."

It took considerable effort on Abigail's part while Mrs. Hadley coached. Mercy took mental notes, knowing it would serve her well in the future. Abigail seemed more worried about Mercy than herself, constantly assuring Mercy that she was alright.

Then, after a moment of desperate effort, there was a cry. A sharp, high-pitched scream broke the tense silence, and Mrs. Hadley lifted a wriggling little body and wrapped it in a towel. Mercy glanced at the bright pink face, it was so tiny, with a tiny nose, lips, and ears.

"It's a little girl," Mrs. Hadley said, carrying the baby over to Abigail and laying her in her arms.

Abigail trembled as she looked down on her child. "Isn't she beautiful, Mercy?"

Mercy smiled. "Just like you, Mama."

"What are you going to call her?" Mrs. Hadley asked.

Abigail frowned. "Henry isn't here to help me decide." She studied her little girl in the dim candlelight, running her fingers over her soft pink skin. "I like Mary, but Henry favored Beth . . ." she said. Then she smiled. "We'll call you Mary-Beth."

"That sounds lovely," Mercy agreed. "Henry will like it too; I know he will."

Abigail closed her eyes momentarily.

"Is she alright?" Mercy asked.

"She came through just fine," Mrs. Hadley said. "She's just tired."

"I would be too," Mercy said with relief.

After everything was complete, and Mrs. Hadley was sure Abigail was no longer in danger, the baby was placed in a bassinet near the bed while Abigail slept. Mercy crawled into bed beside her and pulled the covers up over her shoulders, but she left the candle burning so Abigail could see when she woke to feed the baby. While she lay awake, a wave of relief washed over her and she sobbed tears of relief and gratefulness. Her fears hadn't come true, her mama was alright, they were all alright.

In the morning the boys were permitted to see their new sister, and even Abe couldn't hide how proud he was to hold her. Mercy found herself fascinated by this tiny new person. She seemed to be strong and curious, always looking about as she smacked her tiny lips. Life was unstoppable, even in the middle of a war, life refused to quit.

Abigail wrote to Henry, telling him that all was well, and his second daughter was strong and healthy. Mercy knew he would come to tears the moment he read it; all the best men in her life were courageous but tender on the inside. She wished he could have been there; it was another sacrifice born by many who served. She couldn't wait to watch him hold the little one in his arms, smiling proudly as she knew he would.

This child truly was a gift from heaven, or at least she seemed to be, until about the fourth night. That's when Mercy found herself singing all five verses of Old One Hundredth for three hours straight as she walked laps around the kitchen so Abigail could get some rest. Every time she stopped, Mary-Beth would let her know in no uncertain terms that she wanted her to continue.

By the time the baby fell asleep, Mercy's arms and back were numb, and her feet ached. She laid her in the bassinet and crawled groggily into bed; falling fast asleep before she finished pulling the covers all the way up. It was going to be a short night.

Chapter 25

It wasn't until the end of February that Henry and Benjamin were able to come for a visit. Mercy cried as Henry cried. Cried in joy, and in pain. He had a new baby daughter, his wife was well, but he'd missed the battle and miracle of her birth. He was proud of them, both of them, and thanked the Lord a hundred times. It was the kind of moment that should be immortalized, where everything is raw, and rich, and pure, but the tragedy of such moments is there are no words to describe them accurately, and only those who've lived them can understand them.

Love is like a lion with his cubs. He's the king of all beasts, with terrible might, and claw, and fang, and only a fool would trifle with him. But his cubs may pull his ear, hide in his majestic mane, or pounce on his tail; for their place is a special place, and they know that he wears all the might, and claw, and fang for them.

Love wouldn't be love without the fury and the grace; nor would it be sacred if not tested by fire, nor precious if one didn't have to mine for it in the depths of the soul, but here it was. In the eyes of a father, a proven warrior, a skilled marksman, holding a feeble little child he'd hoped against hope he'd one day see. And she was safe in the arms of the storm because love made it so. And no one dared take her from him.

Mercy let her soul soak it all in, a moment so rare and pure, the magic that flows between a father and his children. The redcoats couldn't win, not against fathers like these, not in a hundred years. The king couldn't stand against the fury and fang, not when it was driven by a love like this. Countless fathers, rising like a storm, driven by love into the thundering tumult of battle against a foe who'd seek to limit the lives of those they cherished.

And she could see it, there, in his eyes . . . he'd never quit. For her, for all of them. He'd rise and rise again, until they were all safe and free, or he'd die trying. It was both beautiful and terrifying, that look in his eyes—the storm. And she thanked the Lord again that He'd placed her under the care of such a man.

Later that afternoon, Henry gathered the family for a meeting. He had that look about him like he always did when he was about to say something he knew wasn't going to be popular with his listeners. He set everyone at the kitchen table, the way he had before they'd moved into the army camp, and after three attempts, began.

"I—I think I'd like you all not to follow Benjamin and I back to the camp this year . . ."

Mercy gasped, looking at Abigail, who didn't meet her gaze.

". . . Things being such as they are, the baby being so young and Abigail still on the mend. I believe the wisest thing to do is use the blessings the Lord has given us, this warm dry tavern, and keep everyone safely here while Ben and I are away."

"But we'll hardly ever see you," David complained.

"I know it will be difficult," Henry agreed. "It will be very difficult. But I feel needlessly putting this child at risk would be negligence on our part."

"What does that mean?" David asked.

"It means, it wouldn't be our best, it wouldn't be love, to put Mary-Beth at risk just to satisfy our own desires."

"Are the Bells going back?" Abe asked.

"Yes, Ben and I will be escorting the Bells back to camp when we go. Mrs. Bell still has Jonathan, and her school."

"Then who will we play with?" David asked.

"There are other children in Cambridge, there were several at the service, some of them used to be your friends before we left, don't you remember?" Abigail asked.

"Yeah . . . But that was a long time ago," David said.

As the shock wore off, Mercy felt a conflict brewing in her heart. She loved working in the tavern, and the living conditions were far better than the camp, but she felt a longing, a calling, back to the men, to the fight, and the service she'd come to love.

"Could I go back with the Bells?" she asked through the din.

The room fell silent as Abigail and Henry looked to one another and then back to Mercy.

"You—you'd be alone, child," Abigail said.

"I know . . . and I know I'd miss you all dreadfully, but—"

"Your place is with the cause," Henry finished.

Mercy nodded, even as tears began to fill her eyes.

"Oh, my sweet child, that is just like you, isn't it?" Abigail said emotionally.

Mercy chewed her lip as their eyes met. "I'm sorry, Mama."

Abigail shook her head, wiping a tear. "Don't be sorry for being the person the Lord called you to be."

"I think I'd like to pray on it," Henry said. "We still have a few days."

Mercy nodded.

"I want to go back too," Abe said.

Henry sighed, placing a hand on Abe's shoulder. "I need a young man like you here to watch over our family while I'm away. I can't think of anyone I'd trust more than you."

"Yes, sir," Abe mumbled, hanging his head.

"What about me?!" David asked.

"Yes, and you too," Henry smiled, patting him on the shoulder.

"And when do I get to fight?" Abe muttered.

Henry turned back to him. "I had Benjamin wait until he was fifteen, and I think it is right you do the same. It's only a year more; if the war isn't yet over, we'll talk about it then."

"Who are you to tell me what to do?!" Abe retorted. "You're not my papa, you've got your own family now, you don't need us. . . ."

"Abraham!" Abigail gasped.

Throwing back his chair, Abe pushed past Henry, and out the door.

"I'll go get him," Benjamin said, making for the door.

"No," Henry caught his arm. "Let him go. He's just a boy processing a lot of hard things . . . and I haven't been there for him."

"Henry, that's not fair," Abigail objected.

"No, it's not. But it's the truth. As a boy becomes a man, he needs a father to show him the way, and Abe's been abandoned twice. I'll find him and talk with him later, but his hurt and fears are no fault of his own. God end this pitiful war." Henry shook his head.

"He didn't mean it," Mercy said. "I had the same fear when I first heard Abigail was going to have her own child . . . I thought you wouldn't need us anymore."

Henry frowned. "We didn't take you in because we needed you or because you needed us. We took you in because we saw you all as a gift from God, and we still do. Mary-Beth is just another gift, but she is no more dear to me than any of you. I'm sorry if we've led you to believe otherwise."

"No," Mercy said. "It was my own foolish imaginations; I should have done better than to doubt your love for us. I feel ashamed now that I can see things as they are."

"After all you children have endured. . . ." Henry sighed. "I'll ever endeavor to assure you of my love and affection for you all."

"As will I," Abigail agreed.

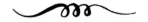

It was through many tears that Mercy and Abe set off with the Bells at the end of Henry's leave. Abe was still plenty sore, and Abigail reckoned there was less of a chance of him runnin' off and joining the cause on his own if he was allowed to come along. Henry would try to find him a place where he could serve but be kept out of the fray. Mercy would continue her service on the medical staff under whomever took Capt. Davis's place, assuming they'd have her.

The year ahead would surely stretch her beyond anything she'd yet to endure, and even as the tavern slipped from view, she wrestled with her decision to return to camp. Her heart already longed for Abigail, David, and Mary-Beth, as a deepening awareness of her loneliness set in. Were it not for the comfort of Adelaide, she probably would have thrown herself from the wagon and run straight back to Abigail.

But there was something else too, an excitement; she'd never been so independent. She'd never had to truly test her capabilities on her own. Of course, she wasn't entirely on her own, Mrs. Bell would keep a watchful eye on her, but for the most part she'd have to learn to take care of herself. The crazy thing was . . . she was confident she could do it.

"Don't slouch, Mercy," Mrs. Bell called across the wagon. "It's bad for your back and even worse for your character."

Mercy nodded and sat up straighter.

Mrs. Bell frowned. "Hmm. Abigail has entrusted you to me, and while in my care I intend to make a lady out of you."

Mercy forced an awkward smile and nodded again.

"I truly wish we could have left that bird in Cambridge," Mrs. Bell muttered. "Stubborn creature has a mind of its own."

Mercy looked to where Theo sat between Ben and Adelaide on the buckboard and smiled to herself.

"You're slouching again!"

Mercy clenched her jaw as she sat up. This was going to be a very long trip.

When they arrived in camp, things got even more interesting. After the wagon was settled, Mercy and Adelaide set off to introduce themselves to the new camp doctor. When they arrived at the field hospital, Mercy entered. There, sitting behind Capt. Davis's desk, was a grizzly bearded man, somewhere in his forties. Upon seeing them, he stood from his desk and hobbled his way over on a peg leg.

"You must be Miss Mercy and Miss Adelaide, I presume."

"Yes, sir," Mercy answered.

"Don't bother calling me sir. I was no officer when I lost my leg."

"Excuse me for asking, but how does a doctor lose his leg?" Mercy asked.

"I was a soldier," the man said. "I lost my leg up at Saratoga, under General Arnold. I had nothing better to do while I mended so I read the doctor's books. The general said we were short on surgeons, so here I am. Flint Musgrave is my name."

"Forgive me, Mr. Musgrave, but you've *never* been a doctor before?" Mercy asked.

"I read the books; didn't you hear me?"

"Yes, sir," Mercy sighed.

"Besides, that boy, uhh, Capt. Davis, he said that you two ladies and a, uhh, Mrs. Tewksbury, were more than capable."

"Mrs. Tewksbury recently had a baby and will no longer be joining us," Mercy said.

"Well, we'll just have to do with what we have," the man said, scratching his beard. "As you can see, we've had a nasty bout with the fever and the pox while you were away, there's plenty to go around."

"We'll fetch our aprons," Mercy said, giving the man a curtsy.

"I'm glad you came back," Adelaide whispered as they dawned their aprons.

"We'll be alright," Mercy said, confidently, though inside she was fighting back her own urge to panic. Truly, this was going to be a difficult year for her diary.

Chapter 26

March 4, 1779

My Dear Friend,

I was relieved beyond words to hear you have returned to camp to assist Mr. Musgrave. These are difficult times indeed and we must all make do with what we have. I hope he can be as humble a student as you were to me and learn quickly, for many lives will depend on it. You are more than capable of handling any of the tasks that will befall you, apart from amputation, which, given our poor results, no one has yet mastered. Perhaps Mr. Musgrave, being a rare success story himself, will have more insights into that practice than you or I. It could very well be that this is all God's grace.

I sympathize with your loneliness, though I can offer you no comfort. It doesn't seem to better with time, or at least in my case it has not. You all gave me the home I thought I'd never have again, and that is where my heart longs to be. If returning to you unharmed at the end of this conflict is my only reward, it would be far more than *enough compensation, and a greater treasure than I could ever hope to find.*

As for the war, we had a great victory at the battle of Kettle Creek, defeating a Loyalist militia marching to reinforce Augusta. The victory was so sound that the British have evacuated the city. They were nearly double our number, but quick tactics enabled us to turn their flanks. We captured men, much needed supplies, and horses.

Our jubilation has been short lived, however. Just yesterday a cunning British attack at Briar Creek has dealt us the most significant defeat of the southern campaign thus far. We lost over 350 men killed or captured, and twice that are wounded or missing. The attack was so well crafted that first reports say the British suffered only a handful of casualties.

This embarrassing defeat has wreaked havoc on our morale, and the leadership of those in command is being called into question. It'll come as no surprise that an unfortunately high number of desertions has taken place overnight, and our officers are more occupied with dispensing justice on those who fled rather than what to do about the enemy.

The army here is only in its infancy and I fear without proper leadership the king may come away with his southern prize. General Lord Cornwallis and his redcoats march like Goliath with no respect for our feeble attempts to oppose him. I pray Washington and the

Lord do not forsake the South, and that we all remain united in the cause of freedom.

I'm sorry I cannot write to you with gladder tidings. I feel, even as I close this letter, that I have nothing worthy of a friend like you. I wish I could send you a ray of sunlight, or perhaps a blossoming flower; I'd like to learn to be more than just a glorious worm as you once called me, albeit in jest.

You are my dearest friend, Mercy Young, and I pray this letter finds you well.

Tobias Davis

Glossary
of Uncommon or Difficult Words

Adept: Skilled or able in a task or area of life

Ardently: Passionately, with great desire

Bleak: Hopeless, dull, plain

Calculating: Counting the cost, weighing the outcomes or benefits, cunning

Contortions: To scrunch up, fold or bend oddly

Coyly: Crafty, scheming

Decorum: Good manners, respectful

Domain: Territory under one's control

Dominance: To rule or control

Draughts: Checkers

Enlightening: To clarify, to come to an understanding

Fantasies: Extravagant or unrestrained imaginations

Feral: Wild, untamed

Fret: Worry

Haggard: Looking exhausted, wasted, in poor condition, usually after prolonged labor or suffering

Hilt: The handle of a sword or knife

Improprieties: Failure to show due honesty or modesty

Inconvenience: Troublesome or difficult

Involuntary: Against or independent of one's own will

Lustfully: with deep ravenous desire

Merits: Good qualities

Musings: Thoughts, imaginations, contemplations

Nemesis: Sworn enemy

No-man's-land: An empty plot of land between two armies that to cross would likely cost a man his life.

Nonchalance: Without care, indifference

Optimism: Being positive about a situation

Pessimism: Being negative about a situation

Prussian: From the area in and around modern-day Latvia, Lithuania, and Poland

Pungent: Strong, overpowering smell

Quartermaster: Person in the military in charge of supplies

Rapture: Extreme pleasure or excitement

Realism: Looking at a situation or circumstance based on facts and logic, not emotions

Refrain: To hold back

Ruefully: Regretfully, with remorse

Sage Advice: Wise advice, usually from an older, seasoned veteran

Sincere: Honest

Spectacle: A sight to see

Subliminally: Unconsciously, without thinking about it

It's not over yet!

I'd love to help other readers enjoy this book as much as you have. If you'd just take a minute and let them know your favorite scene, how the story impacted you, or what book or author you'd compare it to, it will help other readers find it. It's your best way to show your support for us and we greatly appreciate it!

Just scan this QR code to get to our Amazon Author page, click on the right book, and leave your review!

(Even if you purchased or received this copy from somewhere else, you're still eligible to leave a review on Amazon if you have an active account.)

Get your FREE Gifts from J. E. Ribbey!

FREE Story Quiz for Deceptive Victory
with a separate answer key!

FREE Printable Maps
of the Battle of Monmouth

To get these FREE resources and to find out what happens next to Mercy and her family, scan the QR code or visit our website at JERibbey.com!

About the Author

J.E. Ribbey, a husband & wife team, deploys a compelling writing style, combining a fast-paced action thriller with deep character immersion, giving readers an edge-of-your-seat adventure they will feel in the morning. A combat veteran, outdoorsman, and survival enthusiast, Joel enjoys mingling his unique experiences and expertise with his passion for homesteading and the self-sufficient lifestyle in his writing. A homeschooling mom, homesteader, and digital designer, Esther brings the technical, editorial, and design skills to the author team. Together with their four kids they manage a small farmstead in Minnesota, where, besides taking care of the animals and gardens, they also run an event venue and small campground. If you'd like to know more, you can find the Ribbeys on Instagram @j.e.ribbey or at their website JERibbey.com.

Made in the USA
Monee, IL
10 October 2024

67597013R00138